"We have a visitor,"  a mortal."

"Mortal?" Fiona rose that hides Ancient Oaks is

Lana pulled Fiona to the window. A set of wings were tucked into the fairy's back. "See."

Standing on the sidewalk, a man looked at the bookstore. His gaze drifted to Fiona, who gawked at him from the window. Smiling, he gave a small wave. As if a thousand butterflies had been let loose, her middle filled with fluttering.

Was there something about the man?

"Does he look familiar to you?" Fiona asked Lana.

"No, but I can be his new best friend."

The man strode through the bookshop's door and Fiona's fingers began to tingle.

"May I help you?" she asked.

"And if she can't," Lana interjected. "I can."

The man had the good manners to laugh, not leer. "I visited Ancient Oaks years ago with my grandfather." He inhaled. "He met with people in this store. I know it's a long shot, but would anyone remember him?"

Her interest was piqued. "What's your grandfather's name?"

"Rupert Balan."

The frenzied fluttering in her belly ceased. If this man was the grandson of Rupert Balan, it meant one thing. The man was Carter Balan—the first boy Fiona ever kissed.

As Above, So Below

by

Jennifer D. Bokal

As Above, So Below

Cover Art by *Debbie Taylor*

The Wild Rose Press, Inc.
PO Box 708
Adams Basin, NY 14410-0708
Visit us at www.thewildrosepress.com

Publishing History
First Edition, 2021
Trade Paperback ISBN 978-1-5092-3998-6
Digital ISBN 978-1-5092-3999-3

Published in the United States of America

Dedication

To John: Without you, there is no magic in my world.

Prologue

October 31, 1752
Uncharted Territory
Colony of New York, British North America

The wolf understood pain. His whole body throbbed, and a fiery anguish filled each step. An arrow protruded from his back haunches. His fur was matted with dried blood. Night had fallen hours ago, and his black pelt matched the darkness.

He suffered from more than agony. Hours of running left him exhausted.

Dropping down at the base of an old oak tree, he turned his nose to the wind. Dried leaves. The musky scent of a skunk on the other side of the valley. But he could no longer smell the pursuers—the fire from their torches or the hatred that seeped from their pores.

Looking up, he watched the stars through the trees. A cloud passed in front of the moon. His breath caught in his chest and his eyes drifted closed. Here, beneath the branches, would be a good place to die. Especially since his sacrifice meant that everyone else was safe.

Fixing his gaze on the moon, the wolf made ready to breathe his last.

A set of feet landed on the ground in front of him. The wolf too weary to react, glanced upward. He saw a pair of leather shoes, with pewter buckles. Woolen hose.

Petticoats of snowy white. An overdress the color of buttercups and an apron, as blue as the sky on a first warm day of spring. A hand ran through his fur, and he sighed.

"Can you hear me?" *Prudence*. The fairy brought her nose in next to his. Golden hair cascaded over her shoulders and her wide blue eyes held a look of concern. So, she did care for him, at least a little.

Her wings stretched out, shimmering with the starlight. "Hans? Can you hear me? You poor thing. You've been shot. You're exhausted." Her voice held the sing-song lilt of her home in County Cork. Sitting on the ground, she lifted the wolf's head and laid it in her lap. Scratching him behind the ear, she cooed, "Poor dear."

The wolf felt himself slipping away. Poetic, really, to die in the arms of his unrequited love. For it was written that the fae shall never lie with the wolf.

Prudence touched the arrow in his haunches. The white-hot poker of pain ripped through his leg. The wolf was alive now, and once again filled with anguish. He snarled. She petted his muzzle. "Calm yourself, Hans. The others are on their way. They'll take care of the arrow. Rest now, and soon all will be well…"

Then, the fairy pulled the arrow free.

Hans roared and sat up. The night air chilled his skin, and he trembled with the cold. It was then that he realized he no longer was the wolf—nor was he wearing any clothing.

"I didn't mean to… I didn't realize…." Prudence stood quickly and turned her back on his nakedness. Unclasping her cloak, she held it out to him. "Here. Wear this."

He slipped the garment around his shoulders as a

dozen people broke through the underbrush.

"I found him," said Prudence, brightly. "I told you I would."

"Good work," said Goody Moon a stout woman of five and thirty years, with round hips and a round face. A tendril of russet hair clung to her cheek which she tucked beneath her mob cap. "Both of you."

"Hans was shot." Prudence held up the arrow. "In the arse."

"Not my arse." The words came out a growl. The voice was always the last thing to change. He stood. The cheek of his buttock was still filled with the same fiery pain. True, the wolf had been shot in the haunches. But the wound on the man was, well, in the arse.

"Let's see then." Goody Moon, fists on hips, she lifted her chin. "Show me where you were shot."

"Here?" Hans cast a nervous glance at those who gathered "Now?"

"Goodwife." James, Goody Moon's husband stepped forward. He wore a pair of breeches, hose and waistcoat—all in black. The dark clothes helped him to blend with the night. "The lad is discomfited with being unclothed."

Goody Moon harrumphed. "This is hardly the time or place for distress about nakedness—especially since that mob is still out there, somewhere."

It was the mob that set the group to running. There had been rumors for years in the mortal world that magical folks lived in the village outside of Albany. But for a generation, the town had existed in relative peace. In all that time, local mortals visited for comfits and herbs to heal the sick and aide the lovelorn. Then the King in England sent a new governor to the colony of

New York. The governor was one of those horrible kind of men who were bent on destroying everything they couldn't control. The village was the first to be attacked.

Most had escaped. But they'd escaped to go where? Like Moses in the desert, those born of magic, were without a homeland.

"The mob." Prudence echoed. "I'll take a look and see what I can."

Wings fluttering, she rose from the ground and Hans's chest tightened. Now that Goody Moon was here, she'd set him to right. That meant he'd survive, but in surviving he had to live without Prudence. Maybe it would have been better if he died while the fairy stroked his fur.

Prudence's shadow shone against the dark sky. He watched her from the ground and his heartbeat raced like a runaway stallion. His mouth went dry, and his hands ached with the need to touch her.

"There's a waterfall that feeds a creek." Prudence, still suspended in the sky, turned in a slow circle. "It leads to a lake. This valley is shielded on both sides by mountains."

"The mob." James Moon called up to the fairy. "Do you see the mob?"

Prudence descended in a lazy circle, and her feet touched the ground. "There is no sign of the mob. But this valley is well hidden. I don't think they'll find us here."

Hans looked over his shoulder. The magical townsfolks had moved from the base of the oak tree and now sat on the ground. Children rested on the laps of their parents. Husbands held the hands of their wives. Eyes were ringed with dark circles that spoke of exhaustion—of both the body and the mind. Mouths pulled into thin lines. Faces smudged with dirt and ash. They'd all come from different places in the old world to this new land that promised freedom and prosperity for all. It had been a lie. And Hans couldn't help but wonder—now what?

He stepped toward the group. A pain shot through his leg and he growled.

"If you weren't so stubborn," said Goody Moon. "I could fix that arse of yours."

"Goodwife," James said. "Leave the lad be."

"You say leave him be, but what happens when the wound putrefies? Are we to carry this braw lad through the woods whilst being chased by reckless mortals?"

"She's right," said Hans. If the town had to keep moving, he'd be nothing but a burden if he was wounded. "But we should let the shadows hide us, at least."

"Here." James held out a bundle of cloth to Hans. "It's all I could grab quickly from your cottage. A pair of breeches. Hose. Shoes. A shirt."

"Thank you, kindly," he said, taking the clothes and moving to the far side of the tree. He limped with each step. Once sure the darkness hid him properly, Hans lifted the cloak. His face burned with mortification.

Goody Moon lifted her palms to the sky.

"Radiant health blessed be.

Remove that beneath the skin,

That which we cannot see

And bring healing from within."

As if he had a fire to his back, his arse warmed.

Goody Moon repeated, "Radiant health blessed be.

Remove that beneath the skin,

That which we cannot see

And bring healing from within."

The pain in his leg eased and he set his foot on the ground.

Goody Moon chanted her incantation once more.

"Radiant health blessed be.

Remove that beneath the skin,

That which we cannot see

And bring healing from within."

The last of the discomfort slipped away, like water through cloth.

Standing upright, Hans sighed. "Thank you."

Goody Moon nodded. "You can thank me and this tree. The oak is old and has the power of the forest. Come. Let's go before that mob finds us and there are too many holes for me to patch up."

Hans was tired of running and hiding. He'd done both his whole life; beginning in the Black Forest where he was born. In British America, he hoped that things would be different. He knew things could be different— but only if he had the courage to make it so. Did he possess that kind of bravery?

"Goody Moon, how much power is in this tree?" Still under the cloak, Hans slipped on the pair of breeches and buttoned the front fall.

She patted the rough trunk. "Quite a bit. You'd be surprised."

"Maybe we shouldn't run anymore. Maybe we should claim our stake in this new world here and now." He looked around. Yes, this was the perfect place. There was fresh water from the mountains. Game in the woods. Fish in the lake.

"That's a lovely idea, lad. But the mortals would find us eventually. You know that they always do."

"What if they couldn't?" he asked quickly. "What if we were hidden?"

In a flash, he saw a look of understanding in her eyes. "Like behind a veil of magic?"

Hans was a simple werewolf. He knew the cycles of the moon and never dabbled in the art of magic. Yet, he'd seen enough of the witches to know how their craft worked. "Could you cast that kind of a spell?"

"It's possible," said Goody Moon slowly. "But it takes more magic than what I possess."

Hans placed his palm on the tree. "More magic than this ancient oak?"

Goody Moon smiled slowly. "You know lad, you might have just come up with the only way we can all live in peace."

Chapter 1

October 23
Modern Day
Somewhere in the Adirondack Mountains, New York

If only Carter Balan could ignore the nightmare. If only he didn't suspect that there was more to learn about his grandfather's mysterious death from 30 years ago. If only he could convince himself that it was all caused by stress, then he'd never have wasted a perfectly good Saturday looking for a town that wasn't even big enough to warrant a dot on a map.

Thick woods lined both sides of the road. Aside from trees, their leaves changing from green to rust and gold and garnet with the season, he saw nothing. The car crested a ridge. Pulling off the road, he lifted the polaroid from the passenger seat. The image, faded with time, was the last picture ever taken of Carter with his grandfather. Even now, he could see the resemblance—dark hair, dark eyes, olive complexion, Romanesque nose.

Carter, a kid of 13, gave a wide smile that showed a mouthful of braces. Grandfather Balan stared straight at the camera, not a hint of emotion. What had his grandfather been thinking in that moment?

If it weren't for the note on the bottom of the frame—Ancient Oaks, New York, July 10th—Carter would've thought the reoccurring nightmare nothing more than a bad dream. Certainly, Carter had more than enough stress in his life to bring on a night terror or two. Right now, he was on a temporary duty at Fort Drum. When that ended, he was faced with an impending retirement from the Army.

Then again, the picture was proof that Ancient Oaks existed. What's more, he'd been there.

So, the dream meant what? Were the images that came to him at night truly memories and not imagination? He had a vivid recollection of accompanying his grandfather on a business trip to a small town in the mountains of New York. Oddly enough, he remembered some of the landmarks and they led him to, well, the middle of nowhere. Working his jaw back and forth, he exhaled. "The town's gotta be close."

This far into the wilderness, the car's GPS didn't work. Cellular coverage was also non-existent. A roadmap sat on the passenger seat. Carter found his approximate location. Scanning the area for the hundredth time, he looked for two words. Ancient Oaks.

Nothing.

Only a crazy person would keep looking. Carter Balan was many things, but crazy wasn't one of them. He was an Army Doc. He was patriotic and loved his country. Since Uncle Sam had been kind enough to pay for his medical school, Carter returned the favor by serving fifteen years in the Army.

Then again, maybe it *was* a stress dream. Months earlier, he'd been in a combat zone. Upon returning to the states, he decided to retire. Paperwork had been filed. In a few weeks, he'd be a civilian. Carter had dedicated his life to the military and medicine. Hell, he sacrificed his marriage to the long hours demanded by both. At 43 years of age, he couldn't help but wonder—what came next?

Actually, he did know what came next. By turning back now, he could be on base before cocktail hour at the Officer's Club even started.

Tossing both the map and picture onto the passenger seat, he pulled onto the road.

Yet, a sour taste filled his mouth. Tightening his grip on the steering wheel, he glanced out the window. The trees faded and Carter's mind turned—as it always did nowadays—to the nightmare.

Lost in a bank of fog, his grandfather's voice swirled through the mist. "Find me in Ancient Oaks." That first night, he woke sweating and tangled in his sheets, certain someone was watching him as he slept. He checked every inch of his quarters, no one was there.

He couldn't help but wonder, if he gave up the search for Ancient Oaks now, would he forgive himself later? Then again, what else was there to do?

Nothing—and that was the point.

After pulling back onto the pavement, he dropped his foot onto the accelerator. The car shot down the road. It took a moment for his mind to comprehend what his eyes had seen. He slammed on the breaks. The map flew from the seat. Tires shrieking, the acrid stench of burnt rubber filled the air.

Gearshift in reverse, he backed up and stopped. How had he missed it before? There, plain as day, was a wooden sign. Ancient Oaks. Three miles.

"What in the hell?" he whispered.

Trees grew on either side of the narrow road. In the distance, a covered bridge straddled a stream. Beyond, the pavement unfurled like a gray ribbon before disappearing around a bend. He looked back to the road in front of him, it stretched out long and boring—but safe all the same.

Scooping up the map, he dropped it onto the seat. The picture still lay on the floorboard. Somehow, he owed it to his grandfather to make this pilgrimage.

"Three miles," he said, tucking the photo into the pocket of his flannel shirt. "That's not too far. I can be on base before cocktail hour is over."

Turning the steering wheel, Carter drove toward Ancient Oaks, and whatever answers were there for him to find.

****

Fiona Moon stood in the middle of *Rosemary's Bookshoppe.* A box of books, donated to the store after the death of a warlock from Denver, sat in the middle of the room. Nearby, Emerson, a black and white cat lazed near the window.

Bookshelves, from floor to ceiling, filled three of the four walls. Several round tables sat near a window that overlooked Ancient Oak's Main Street. A beverage caddy—complete with cups, a pot of hot water and cannisters of loose tea—sat near the door. Toward the back of the shop, half of a dozen rectangular tables were piled high with various titles.

The store was just as it had been when Fiona's great-great-grandmother, Rosemary Moon, had gone into business. Same as the store, not much had changed in the town of Ancient Oaks. For centuries, it had been a place for magical folks who wanted to live apart from the mortal world. It's not that Fiona minded things always being the same. Nor did she mind that her family was preeminent in the town's history. Honestly, she liked being the town's Book Witch—taking the same job as her parents, and the parents of her parents—and on and on for generations. It's just that sometimes she wished something would happen to make one day stand out from the next.

The morning shoppers had gone home for lunch and the evening browsers had yet to emerge. The quiet didn't bother Fiona. She had plenty to keep her busy—what with all the new books to be sorted.

She scanned the street beyond the window. The sky filled with dark clouds. A gust of wind sent leaves skittering down the street. Certainly, there'd be rain before nightfall.

Like drunken dancers, the leaves swirled past a lamp post with cornstalks attached before moving past a scarecrow affixed to the outside wall of the candy shop. The scent of donuts, freshly baked, was carried on the wind and seeped into the store. On the hills, the hardwood trees had changed their summer greens for the autumnal colors of gold, orange, and red.

Pressing her palms against the glass, Fiona couldn't help but smile. Fall was her favorite time of the year. It wasn't just the colors, scents and sounds of the season that she loved either.

Halloween was little more than a week away. At this time of year, magic was everywhere. Her heart raced, and her fingers tingled. How long had it been since she cast a proper spell?

Weeks? More like months. Certainly, she could tap into the power that flowed freely. Maybe now was the time to try again.

Fionna set the box of books in front of her. Her

auburn hair fell in loose waves over her shoulders. Gathering up her tresses, she quickly secured them into a bun at the nape of her neck. Inhaling, Fiona rolled her shoulders and her wrists.

"Concentrate. Concentrate. Concentrate," she said, with her exhale.

In her mind's eye, she saw the books in the box sorting themselves throughout the store. Inhale. Exhale. She allowed her breath to set the rhythm. Planting her feet firmly on the worn floor, she held her hands at her side and stretched her fingers wide.

"As above and so below
Rains will come and rivers flow
Sun will shine and winds will blow
Books will rise and know where to go."

The tingling in her fingers grew until her palms vibrated with an unseen force. In her mind, Fiona saw tendrils of blue light reaching from her hands to touch the books.

On the floor, the box trembled.

Narrowing her eyes, her vision blurred until she could see the crack between the physical and magical worlds. A gray mist surrounded the carboard box, thickening until the whole box sparkled with silver.

"As above and so below
Rains will come and rivers flow
Sun will shine and winds will blow
Books will rise and know where to go."

The light grew brighter, and the box rocked from side to side. Her hands warmed and sweat collected on her brow and at the nape of her neck.

She inhaled again, drawing magic up through the soles of her feet. She brought down magic from above, making herself a conduit to the power. Exhaling, she recited the incantation for a third and final time,

"As above and so below
Rains will come and rivers flow
Sun will shine and winds will blow
Books will rise and know where to go."

A gale blew through the store, fluttering the box flaps with the force of the wind. Fiona's chest expanded with pride and hope. She'd done it again. After all this time—she'd harnessed her power. Then, like a light bulb exploding, a pang shot through her chest. The gust stopped. The energy was gone. Her magic had vanished.

Her eyes stung and watered. Fiona was the Daughter of the Moon. It was a title that dated back to the founding of Ancient Oaks, when her great grandmother seven generations back had draped a spell over the town, like camouflage. Since then, the magical folk had lived safely hidden from the mortal world. Yet, now, all these centuries later, was Fiona to be the first in her family to fail?

A single tear leaked down her cheek. Biting the inside of her lip hard, she refused to cry. Sobbing would change nothing.

In the silence of the book shop, she had to be honest—even if it were just to herself. It hadn't been merely weeks or months since she'd last wielded magic. It had been years. Over two years, in fact. She hadn't used magic properly since just before her 40th birthday.

Oh sure, she'd made the odd cup of tea from nothing but an empty mug. At the town's 4th of July picnic, she conjured sparks with the tips of her fingers—and even that was a struggle.

Oh, you know the problem, whispered a voice inside

her head. *It's your age. You're too old. Magic is for the young. The fresh. The pretty.*

Moving to the window, Fiona brought to mind a dozen witches or warlocks who did magic in old age. Rachel. Tad. Her parents—though they'd retired and now lived in the mortal world.

The voice came again. *Magic is for the young or the formidable. You're neither and that's why your power has gone. Imagine that, Daughter of the Moon—the line of your family magic ends with you.*

As a child, Fiona had been taught to ignore her inner critic. It's just that the voice had become a constant companion. Was the critic right? Was her magic gone?

No. She could still cast a spell. It's simply that she hadn't been practicing enough lately, that's all. Certainly, she could still create a ball of light. Breathing deeply, Fiona stood tall and placed her palms close, cupping her hands. A spark of blue flame collected in the space. She closed her eyes and imagined a marble fountain in the middle of her chest. Light, not water, flowed from the fountain and Fiona channeled it to the spark.

Power moved through her veins, her bones, her muscles. Her arms ached. Her head pounded. Gritting her teeth, she focused. The light in her hand grew into a sphere. It pulsed and pressed against her fingers, trying to break free.

She opened her hands. Emerson watched as the ball floated to the ceiling. Sighing with relief, Fiona relaxed. Then, like a bubble, the ball of light popped and was no more.

"Damnit," she cursed. If she couldn't wield her magic, what was she? Could she even call herself a

15

witch?

She had to do something else. But what?

For now, there was a box of books that needed to be sorted. After that, well, if Fiona were to be completely honest—she didn't know what came next.

Maybe, that was the problem.

Returning her attention to the donated books, she picked up a leather-bound tome, with a brass latch. She read the title: Diary of a Vampire Hunter by Rupert Balan.

Rupert Balan. Now that was a name she hadn't heard in years. She recalled the day he'd come to Ancient Oaks. It was mid-July and Fiona had been weeks from her 13th birthday. She couldn't recall the reason for the visit, but since the meeting took place at the bookstore, she'd been tasked with keeping his grandson—a gangly youth with braces—company.

Flipping through the pages, yellow with age, she stopped and read a passage.

"The Vampire dates back to the time of the gods. A creation of Mars—the god of war, the Vampire was meant to bring destruction to the world. More than being immortal, the Vampire's saliva holds a toxin that, when introduced to the bloodstream, the victim becomes one of the undead."

Holding a hand over the worn, leather cover she let the book's energy fill her. Fiona heard rushing water and then, a scream. A shiver ran down her spine and lifted the hairs on her arm. She set the book aside and returned to the cash register. On the counter was a forgotten mug of apple cider. Fiona took a sip and grimaced. The cider had cooled and was tepid, yet taking a drink helped to calm her nerves.

A set of bells above the door tinkled as Lana Gold, Fiona's best friend since forever, flitted across the threshold. Emerson looked up, blinked, yawned, and lay back down.

Lana wore a pale, yellow sweater with a low back, that matched the color of her hair. It accentuated her friends willowy frame and made her large blue eyes all the bluer. In fact, she almost shimmered.

Fiona tugged her black sweatshirt lower over her black leggings and wished that she would have done something with her wavy red hair, besides twist it into a messy bun.

"What're you doing?" Lana asked, flicking her fingers toward the box of books.

"These?" Fiona held up a dog-eared paperback book. *Grimm's Fairytales.* "They came from a warlock's estate. The family sent them to me."

"No." Lana asked, "What are you doing? Can't you cast a spell or something to make all of those go where they belong?"

Kneeling next to the box, Fiona rummaged through the titles. "I like books. The way they feel. Smell. Besides, I need to examine them first..." It was a lie, sure. Still, it was tinged with some truth.

"So," Fiona began. "What're you up to?"

"I have the best news."

On second thought, her friend really was shimmering. Then again, fairies did shimmer when they were excited. "The best news," Fiona echoed, curious. "What is it?"

"We have a visitor," said Lana. "He's so handsome. And he's *mortal.*"

"Mortal?" Fiona rose to her feet. "No way. The spell

that hides Ancient Oaks is too strong. No mortal could ever find the road." She didn't bother to add that even if a mortal arrived in town, they were to be sent away as soon as possible. Even though the days of mobs with pitchforks and torches had ended, Ancient Oaks adhered to a strict "No Mortals Allowed" policy.

"Come here." Lana pulled Fiona toward the window. A set of wings were tucked tight into the fairy's back, the outline translucent against her skin. "See."

A red car cruised past, slowing as it neared a pile of more than 100 pumpkins that were waiting to be carved into jack-o-lanterns. The driver was visible through the window and Fiona's heart skipped a beat. He had dark hair, dark eyes, and one of those profiles that could make a girl go weak in the knees—even if she wasn't really a girl anymore.

"That's a mortal all right. How'd you think he found us?"

"I don't know," said Lana, with a clap. "Maybe he has a magical branch in his family tree. He's dark and sexy. I say he's part werewolf."

"It doesn't matter even if he is part magic, he has to go. You know that's the rule."

After parking his car on the corner, the man stepped onto the sidewalk. As Fiona had noticed earlier, he was handsome. Yet, that term didn't quite do him justice. He was tall with broad shoulders. He wore a dark blue flannel shirt that hugged his well-muscled chest and biceps. A pair of jeans accentuated his rear. At the sight of him, Fiona's mouth went dry.

"If I knew that mortals looked *that* good, I'd leave Ancient Oaks a little more often," Lana purred.

Fiona glanced at her friend. "I thought you swore off

the mortal world forever."

"I did," said Lana. "But now I understand that tequila and ice cream don't mix."

Standing on the sidewalk, the man scanned the shops that lined the road. His gaze stopped on the bookstore before drifting to Fiona, who still gawked at him from the window. He smiled and lifted his fingers in a small wave. As if a thousand butterflies had been let loose in her stomach, her middle filled with fluttering.

Yet, there was something about the man.

"Does he look familiar to you?" Fiona asked Lana.

"No, but I'd love to be his new best friend."

The man strode through the bookshop's door and Fiona's fingers began to tingle. She didn't dislike the sensation.

"May I help you?" she asked.

"And if she can't," Lana interjected. "I can."

The man had the good manners to laugh, not leer. "I hope so. I visited Ancient Oaks years ago with my grandfather and well." He inhaled. "He met with people in this bookstore. In fact, I remember sitting right at this table and drinking lemonade." He placed his hand on the wooden top, his gaze hazy as he looked into the past. "Huh, I'd forgotten that detail until now." He paused a beat. Emerson rose from his place on the floor and sauntered over to the man. Bending down, the mortal ruffled the fur on the cat's head. "I know it's a long shot, but I was wondering if anyone might remember him."

A grandfather with business in Ancient Oaks? Fiona couldn't help it. Her interest was piqued. Besides, Emerson was a good judge of character. If he trusted the stranger, then she could—at least a little.

She stepped toward the man. The tingling in her

fingers shot up her arm, through her shoulder, before settling in her belly with the excited butterflies. "What was your grandfather's name?"

"Balan," he said. "Rupert Balan."

The frenzied fluttering in her belly ceased. If this man's grandfather was Rupert Balan, then it meant one thing. The man was Carter Balan—the first boy Fiona ever kissed.

Searching his face, she looked for a glimmer of recognition. There was none. Certainly, he hadn't forgotten about her. Unless, he had.

She'd been silent too long. She needed to say something. "And what's your name?" she asked, though she already knew the answer.

"Me? I'm Carter. Carter Balan. I should've introduced myself first. And you are?"

She swallowed. "I'm Fiona Moon, and this is my friend, Lana Gold."

"I've heard of Rupert Balan," said Lana. "He's famous."

Carter drew his brows together in confusion. "My grandfather? He was an architect who specialized in restoring old buildings. How'd that make him famous?"

Did Carter not know anything about his grandfather? His family? For centuries the Balan name was synonymous with vampire hunting. Watching Carter from the side of her eye, she caught a glimpse of a haze surrounding his head. No wonder his thinking was foggy—his memories had been wiped clean. It was a common enough tactic in the uncommon event that a mortal discovered that magic really existed. But if Carter was a Balan, he was part of the magical world. So why erase his adolescent memories? Maybe she should be asking something more important. Why did he now have a vague recollection of visiting Ancient Oaks?

The question of his grandfather's fame still hung in the air—Fiona could almost see the words stuck in Carter's brain fog.

"He's an author," Fiona answered quickly. True, Rupert Balan wasn't known world-wide for his written words, but hadn't she just been reading a book he'd authored? It meant that while she wasn't exactly telling Carter everything, she wasn't lying either.

"He is?" asked Lana.

Fiona shot her friend a glare.

Lana's large eyes got wider as she understood the unspoken warning. "He is," she repeated.

"Really?" said Carter. "I never knew." With a shake of his head, his words trailed off. "I wonder if that's why he came to this bookstore. Think he was here for a book signing?"

Fiona shrugged. "Possibly."

"It's just." Shaking his head, he gave a wry laugh. "It's just that my grandfather died right after the visit. I'm not completely sure what I'm looking for—but I'd like to speak to someone who was around that day."

Was Carter simply looking for closure?

Fiona glanced out the window. A bank of storm clouds hung low in the sky. A gust of wind blew, rattling the windows and ripping the wreath from the door of the candy store. Emerson skittered beneath a bookshelf.

Electricity gathered in the air and danced along her skin. Carter's story about visiting Ancient Oaks with his grandfather was caught in the ozone. Was it because she'd just found a book that was written by his grandfather and that was too much of a coincidence to be much of a coincidence at all?

Or was it because he was the first boy she ever kissed—even if he didn't remember her.

Or maybe she felt because of that single afternoon spent together as adolescents, Carter's history intertwined with her own.

In the end, she decided that it really didn't matter. The rule about not allowing mortals to remain in Ancient Oaks be damned. Fiona was going to help Carter Balan.

Chapter 2

Fiona knew she needed to help Carter Balan. But why? And how?

Then again, there was really only one person who would remember the day that Rupert Balan came to Ancient Oaks.

"Lana, can you mind the store for a few minutes?"

"Sure," said Lana, moving to the counter. "I'm always happy to help."

It's exactly the answer Fiona hoped to hear. "Thanks," she said. "You're the best. If you need to leave before I get back, just put up the *closed* sign." Opening the door, she turned to Carter. "I want you to meet Rachel. If anyone knows about your grandfather, it's her."

"Rachel," he asked, stepping onto the sidewalk. "Who's Rachel?"

She followed. Outside, a crisp breeze blew down from the surrounding mountains. The air smelled of cinnamon and sugar and Fiona wondered what was being prepared at the bakery. All the storefronts were decorated for the upcoming holiday. Some of the businesses chose the mortal way to celebrate Halloween. The dentist's office had a plastic spider, four feet wide, standing outside the door. As they passed, all the eyes seemed to follow Fiona. She paused, hoping that the spider was plastic.

23

The candy shop across the street had chosen more traditional decorations for All Hallow's Eve. Gold, orange and red bunting hung from the eaves to signify the changing colors. Pumpkins, gourds, and misshapen squash sat on hay bales to celebrate the fall harvest.

Fiona took a few steps while wondering how to answer Carter's question. *Who was Rachel?* While his query was simple—the answer was not. Rachel was the most powerful witch in Ancient Oaks. Besides being a member of the town council, the elder witch had the gift of healing and knew everything that happened in town. "She runs the medical clinic," said Fiona. Pointing to a small, white house, surrounded by a picket fence. The building was original to the founding of the town. In fact, the town's magical oak sat in the middle of her yard. "It's right up there."

"Clinic?" Carter repeated. "Is Rachel a doctor, or something like that?"

Rachel was so much more than a mere physician. Over the decades, she'd mastered more than a thousand different spells. "Yeah," Fiona agreed. "She's something like that."

"Interesting. I'm a physician, too."

True, Fiona didn't often use western medicine. Still, she admired the dedication and intellect it took to become a mortal healer. She glanced at him. His hair was short and shaved at the neck. His shoulders were squared and his posture erect. "A doctor, huh? I would have guessed that you were a military man."

He gave a quick laugh. The sound landed like lightning in her belly. "You'd be right about that, as well."

"A doctor and a soldier? Impressive," she said. And

honestly, she was a touch impressed. They approached the clinic. Three people stood on the lawn, gathered in a tight knot of conversation. Whatever they said, was blown away by the breeze.

"There she is," said Fiona to Carter. "That's Rachel. The tall guy is Tad, the mayor of Ancient Oaks. The other man is Dominic, he's Lana's great uncle and can fix about anything."

Before Carter had a chance to respond, Rachel glanced over her shoulder and smiled wide. "Look who the wind blew up the street. What can I do for you, Fiona?" Rachel asked. Her silver hair hung loose around her shoulders and a purple shawl was draped over her arms. She also wore a pair of onyx earrings. "And who's your friend?"

"I'm glad we found you all. This is Carter Balan, Rupert's grandson. He visited Ancient Oaks years ago and has some questions about his grandfather. I was hoping you can help."

"Rupert Balan," Tad repeated. "Now there's a name I haven't heard in years."

Before moving to Ancient Oaks, a decade before, Tad lived in the mortal world and worked as an attorney in New York City. He still wore his hair slicked back and always donned a crisp, white shirt.

"You met Rupert, too?" Fiona asked, genuinely surprised.

"Of course, I did. I was the one who called and asked him to come to town."

"Really?" Carter stepped forward. "Do you remember why?"

"You know," said Rachel, shaking a finger at Carter. "You really do look like Rupert. Don't you think he

25

looks just like his grandfather, Dom?"

Dominic wore a green sweatshirt that read: *Will work for Cheeseburgers* in faded gold script. Leaning against the trunk of the tree, he folded his arms across his chest. Most fairies were born with a pleasant disposition. But not Dominic. Where the usual fairy was happy, he was surly.

"I'm old," he said, with a scowl. "I don't remember much from thirty years ago."

"But you remember that it was thirty years ago," Carter said. His words were part statement, part challenge. "That counts for something."

"I have to go," Dominic grumbled. Pushing off the tree, he shoved his hands in his pockets and stalked off.

Wow. That was abrupt, even for Dominic. Fiona couldn't help but wonder, what got Dom so upset that he had to leave?

"Looks like Dominic's still sore about what happened, even all these years later," said Tad, by way of an explanation. He continued, "There was some trouble with one of the buildings on Main Street. Dom was the town's engineer back in those days. He tried to fix it but couldn't. Rachel called me in the city and asked for help. I knew of your grandfather's reputation and made the call. After a quick chat, he agreed to consult."

Rachel picked up the story. "Your grandfather had some suggestions. Dominic was able to get everything under control, but I think it hurt his pride to ask for outside help."

Fiona didn't remember anything being wrong with one of the buildings. They were built with brick and mortar, sure, but also magic. "Which building?" she asked.

Rachel waved away her question. "Doesn't matter now, dear. Anything else you'd like to know, Carter?"

"How did he seem to you that day? Did anything happen to my grandfather?" he asked.

"Happened to him?" Rachel narrowed her eyes. "Like what?"

Carter rubbed the back of his neck. "It's just that my grandfather died a few days after his visit."

Rachel *tsked.* "I remember hearing about that. Tragic. I'm sorry for your loss, by the way."

Nodding, Carter accepted her condolences. A rumble of thunder rolled down from the hills. A dirt devil swirled across the street.

"Can we help you with anything else?" Rachel asked. "It looks like a storm's about to break. The bridge washes out quickly. I'd hate for you to get stuck."

With a sigh, Carter checked his watch. "You're right, I better get going. Thanks for answering my questions."

"Sure thing," said Tad. "I hope we helped."

With a nod, Carter turned for the path. Fiona paused. A single question clung to her lips, but she dared not ask. Rachel and Tad had lied to Carter. Why? What was it that they were trying to hide?

****

Fiona caught up with Carter and walked at his side. With each step, she looked at Ancient Oaks with a critical eye. After all, it was the first time she'd had a mortal with her in town. True, Fiona had taken Carter Balan to talk to Rachel and the rest of the council. Yet, she was positive that he knew nothing about the town's magical history. What did he see? A small village of 2,000 souls that was in a narrow valley. Main Street, a four-block business district, ran down the seam between the hills. Then those same hills led to distant mountain peaks.

At one end of downtown sat a non-denominational church. At the other end, there was a large stone inn. A park with a gazebo and city hall filled half of a block. Risers were set up around the gazebo, ready to be filled with jack-o-lanterns on All Hallows Eve. A pit, for a bonfire, had already been dug.

All along the street, the buildings were made of red brick. Most of them were three and four stories tall. Neat shops sat cheek to jowl with their neighbor. Her bookstore. Candy's Candies. The dentist's office shared a front door with the office of the local newspaper, commonly called, The Crier. Houses dotted the hills. Beyond those, the woods.

Did he notice anything out of the ordinary?

Sure, Fiona visited the mortal world often. There was much to see. Some of it was amazing, like the skyscrapers in New York City and Chicago. She found Mt. Rushmore to be a true achievement, until she learned that the chief engineer was half fairy.

There were also parts of the mortal world that were less than pretty. Urban rot. Poverty. Crime. Hunger of both the body and the soul. Would he notice that everyone in town was happy and healthy? And if he did, what would he think?

"So." Carter drew out the single word. "Tell me about Ancient Oaks."

The hairs on her arm stood straight. "What do you want to know?"

He shrugged. "It looks like a nice place. What do people do here for a living?"

"This and that." Fiona shrugged. "I run the bookstore. Lana's a teacher. Rachel manages the clinic."

"Is there a Mr. Moon?"

Fiona hadn't blushed in years, yet her face grew warm. "Mr. Moon?" she echoed. "Are you asking about my dad? Or are you trying to figure out if I'm married?"

He laughed. "I was asking about the second one, just not very well."

"No, there is no Mr. Moon—except my father."

"Boyfriend?"

"Nope." How long had it been since a man flirted with Fiona? She couldn't recall the last time—which meant it had been far too long.

"What about you? Is there a Mrs. Balan?"

"There was, but she got sick of me working so much. Hospital shifts are hard on a marriage. Deployments are harder."

"I can imagine," said Fiona. They walked a little more, and the conversation seemed to have run its course. If she wanted Carter to simply leave town, then the wisest thing was to say no more. If that were true, then why did she ask, "Tell me what you remember about your trip to Ancient Oaks?"

Carter, fingertips tucked into the pocket of his jeans, simply shook his head.

She continued, "You found your way here. That's quite a feat, we aren't on any maps." She didn't bother to add that the town was hidden by a spell and few mortals could ever find their way to the town, even if they tried.

His car, a red sedan, sat next to the curb. Using the fob, he started the engine and unlocked the doors. Shaking his head again, Carter sighed. "I guess that's why I came. I don't remember much and yet…" His words trailed off as he scanned the empty street. "I feel like something happened here. Something that I should remember but can't."

Like his first kiss with Fiona? Or was there more?

"Do you think those two, Tad and Rachel, are lying?" He pressed his lips together, as if he'd thought better about what to say but was too late. "Sorry, I'm direct. It's a blessing and a curse."

"I don't know why they wouldn't tell you everything…" Carter might have the last name of Balan, but he was a mortal for sure. For the sake of the town, she needed to send him on his way. "Rachel's right about the bridge. It washes out all of the time."

"You'd tell me if there was more to know, right? I don't have a reason to trust you, but I do."

"Do you have a card or something? I can call if I hear anything."

He removed his wallet and withdrew a white business card. From where she stood, Fiona could see the seal of the United States Army and the words, Major Carter Balan, M.D. He held it out before shaking his head. "Actually, I'm set to retire in a few weeks. All this information—even the cell number—will be useless." Inclining his head to the car, he said, "I better get going."

"Sure," said Fiona, taking a step back. "Have a safe trip."

"Thanks for helping me," he said, his hand resting on the door handle.

"Anytime." She should turn around and go back to her bookstore, her cat, and her boring but predictable life. Yet, she stood on the street. A breeze, like a lover's whisper, blew across the nape of her neck.

"It was nice meeting you," he said, his hand still on the car's door.

There was another part of her—one that was not a witch and only a woman—who studied his profile and wondered what it would feel like to have his lips on her mouth, or at the base of her throat, or on the lobe of her ear.

"Nice meeting you, too." Her mouth was dry, and her voice came out as a croak. Clearing her throat she tried again, "Well, I better." She took another step back, forcing herself to walk away from Carter Balan.

"You know," he began, his words halting her retreat. "Base isn't that far away—at least since I know how to get here. There's a college football game tonight. I could probably get us a pair of tickets if you're interested."

A date? Had Carter Balan just asked her out on a date?

Obviously, he had. Now, she had to make a decision. Go? Decline?

What was she going to say?

****

Dominic had been born with a knack for fixing all things mechanical. Even without training, he understood gears, electricity, and to a lesser amount—computers. It had made him one of the most popular fairies in Ancient Oaks.

Got a clock that's broken? Call Dominic.

Does your toaster always burn the bread? Call Dominic.

Have a car that won't start? Call Dominic.

The paved path toward his house ran straight up the side of a hill, before becoming gravel as the trees grew closer together. Trudging ever upward, he knew there was one problem he couldn't fix. And it had to do with the arrival of Rupert Balan's grandson. Dominic knew the truth. Obviously, Rachel and Tad didn't want to say anything, and he knew why. Maybe none of them held the knife, but still their hands were covered in blood because of what happened that day.

Carter Balan deserved to know what happened all those years ago. A fixer by nature, he wanted to find the mortal and tell him everything. But what was he supposed to say, especially since the truth was so unbelievable?

A breeze rattled through the tree branches and Dominic glanced at the sky. In the distance, storm clouds roiled. "Great," he said. His house was still more than a mile away, tucked deep in the forest. "I suppose I'll have to walk home in the rain."

Walk home in the rain.

Words came to him from the surrounding woods.

Dominic stopped. His blood was already boiling, and he wasn't in the mood to be teased. "Who's there? Is that you Thomas Quincy?" Or maybe a fight was just what he needed. "If it is, I won't worry about talking to your mother, but I'll tan your hide myself."

Tan your hide myself.

"Thomas Quincy, you little snot, if you don't come over here right now, I'm going to get you. Is that what you want? For me to come and get you."

Come and get you.

"That's it." Thomas Quincy—what a little turd. This time Dominic wasn't going to let himself be laughed at or taunted. He strode through the tree line as the first rumble of thunder echoed off the surrounding hills. Inside the woods, behind the clouds, the temperature dropped. Dominic didn't care about the chill in the air. His anger kept him warm. Yet, where was the kid?

The forest told no secrets. An unblemished carpet of decaying leaves covered the ground. There was no sound of childish laughter. No rustling in the bushes, where a lanky kid with freckles might hide.

The first fat raindrop hit the upper branches of the canopy. Then another. And another. The symphony of the storm grew with the cymbal of a lightning strike and the bass of a thunderclap.

A single drop made it through the thick branches above and hit Dominic on the middle of his balding pate.

"Come out now, Thomas. The fun's over. Your mother won't want you out in this storm. I'll help to get you home."

Nothing.

"I promise, I won't tan your hide. I won't even say anything to your mother."

He paused to listen, there were no other sounds beyond the percussion of the rain in the trees.

"Thomas?" Where was the kid? Had he run away? Or had something happened? Dominic called, louder this time, his pulse rising with his concern. "Yell if you can hear me."

Another raindrop fell on his head and another. Dominic wiped them away.

What had he noticed first? The smell—metallic and meaty. Or that the viscosity was thicker and smoother than rainwater?

He looked at his hand. It was covered in red.

Blood?

His breath caught in his chest and the acrid taste of panic coated his tongue.

Hand trembling, Dominic looked up. He'd been wrong about Thomas Quincy being in the woods. What he saw was terrible and his heart seized at the sight.

****

Why in the hell had Carter asked Fiona on a date? His invitation hung between them, like a speech bubble in a comic strip. She was going to refuse. He could tell.

Then again, he didn't blame her.

Fiona knew nothing about Carter, other than he was a stranger with a strange tale about a long-dead grandfather and faded memories. She didn't seem to be the judgmental type, but Carter wouldn't blame Fiona if she thought he was a loon.

It was best if he left Ancient Oaks and never looked back.

Why then, did he stay on the sidewalk, unable and unwilling to move? Why did he loathe the idea of never again seeing Fiona Moon?

"Football?" Fiona shook her head and echoed his offer to take her to a game. "I really don't do sports."

"Dinner, then? You have to eat sometime."

"If the bridge washes out, I won't be able to get back home."

"I understand," he began, "that we just met. You don't know me. You don't know if you can trust me. I get it. But I like you. I'd like to get to know you better."

She dragged her bottom lip through her teeth. He was transfixed by the gesture and his heartbeat in triple-time. It was more than excitement and trepidation about what she might do or say next. It was the woman herself. Of course, he'd noticed that she was attractive— beautiful in an earthy kind of way. Her outfit was simple—only black leggings and a sweatshirt, still the fabric hugged the curves of her body and accentuated her womanly shape. Her blue eyes were large, her lips were coral and somehow all the colors reminded him of a Caribbean sunset.

"You know," she began, drawing out the words. His gaze was drawn to her mouth as his mind filled with images of his lips on hers.

Whatever she was about to say next was cut off by a high-pitched sound. Carter's blood ran cold.

"What was that?" Fiona asked, taking a step closer to Carter.

Using the fob, he silenced the car's engine.

Holding his breath, he strained to listen. What had he heard? "A scream?" he glanced beyond the line of building and into the surrounding forest. "I think it came from the woods."

"An animal? Maybe a rabbit was caught by a fox," she suggested, never mind that a fox was a nocturnal hunter and not likely to be hunting in the middle of the afternoon.

They waited, each silent and still, not even daring to breathe. He scanned the street. It was empty. The woods were silent.

"Maybe it was an animal," he agreed. Still, someone should check out the noise—just to make sure. Before he could ask about any local law enforcement, it came again.

A piercing shriek ripped the quiet afternoon in two.

"That definitely wasn't an animal," said Carter. Hairs at the nape of his neck stood straight.

"It came from over there." Fiona pointed to a narrow path that ran between two buildings. A crumbling set of stone steps led up a hill, before the trail disappeared into the woods.

Carter was running toward the stairs before he even realized that he'd moved.

"Where are you going?" Jogging, Fiona caught up with him.

"Someone in the woods is hurt. I need to find them and help." He placed his foot on the first step. Fiona stood on the sidewalk, biting her bottom lip. Her brows were drawn together, and he tried to guess her mood. Concerned? Uneasy? Distressed? Without her having to say a word, he knew she was scared. Still, the need to act was keen. "You stay here. Find the doctor—Rachel. Then, call the police. Either way, someone needs help and I'm going to go and find them." Looking back to the tree line, he couldn't help but wonder who'd screamed and why?

"I can't let you go by yourself. What happens if you get lost?" Folding her arms across her chest, Fiona started running up the steps. "I hate the woods, but I'll come with you."

A typical fall afternoon in the Adirondack's, a dark wall of clouds hung over the southern horizon. In the distance, a fork of lightning split the sky in two. Like an army marching across the land, within minutes the storm would be upon them.

With Fiona at his side, they quickly ascended the stairs. Standing at the edge of the woods, Carter paused. Pulse pounding in his ears, he glanced at Fiona. Her cheeks were ruddy with exertion.

"You ready?" he asked.

She shook her head. "But I'm going anyway." She crossed the tree line and he followed.

The forest was quiet. Trees grew for miles. Tall and

narrow, he could imagine the oaks and maples as silent sentinels. Dried leaves carpeted the ground. Carter scanned the woods.

Yet, what was he looking for?

His gaze stopped.

"What's that?" Fiona asked. Obviously, she'd seen it, too.

Two yards ahead, a pile of leaves had been flipped over, showing the damp underbelly. The scrape was the right size to be a footprint. A few feet further, a broken twig lay on the ground. "It's not exactly a trail of breadcrumbs." He turned his nose to the wind, like a dog trying to catch a scent. The action surprised him—and yet, he thought he might smell something. But what? "But it's easy enough to follow."

Adrenaline coursed through his system, an electric charge that allowed him to see and hear everything. Overhead, rain began to fall. Drops hit the uppermost branches with a soothing percussion. They were headed in the right direction. He could feel it in his bones.

"Someone's definitely been here," Fiona said, her voice little more than a whisper. "You think they're the ones who screamed?"

"Let's keep going and find out."

They passed a copse of trees. It was there, at the base of a spindly maple tree. Black as tar, a puddle covered the ground. Fiona gasped.

Instinctively, he stepped in front of her—shielding her from the gore.

"Is that?" Fiona paused. "Blood?"

"I think it is," he said, swallowing down his alarm.

She asked, "Is it from a human? Maybe the scream we heard was just a predator and prey."

It was a reasonable question. Then again, that was a lot of blood for something small, like a rabbit.

He saw it from the corner of his eye first. There, on the pale trunk of a tree, was a bloody handprint.

****

The storm began to rage. The overhead canopy did little to stop the deluge. Raindrops pelted Fiona's face. Cold water ran in rivulets down the back of her shirt, until the fabric clung to her skin. Her chest was tight, and her throat was raw. Yet, all she saw was the red outline of a hand on the white trunk of a tree.

What the hell happened?

"Just breathe." Carter placed his hand on her shoulder. "Inhale. Exhale. Breathe."

She followed his directions and the cords of anxiety around her chest loosened.

"I…" she began, not sure how she could explain that more left her unnerved than the bloody handprint—although that was more than enough. In the forest, she felt exposed. It was as if eyes watched her from behind every tree. She glanced over her shoulder before turning back to Carter. "I'm fine now."

"Are you sure?" Carter held out his hand.

She slipped her palm into his. His touch was warm and reassuring. "Maybe we should get the police chief, Porter." Porter had been Fiona's friend since birth, and he was a heck of a cop. He was tough, fair, loyal, plus—he could smell a lie.

"That's a good idea." Carter squeezed Fiona's hand tighter, before letting her palm slip from his grasp. "You go back to town and get the police. There's more underbrush that's been turned over. I want to follow the trail before this storm washes away whatever clues thare

38

to find."

Her gaze darted to every tree. Was someone—or something—lurking behind a trunk? Was she ready to be alone in the woods? Or maybe she should be asking another question. Was she really going to let her fear get in the way of helping someone who was obviously hurt?

"I'll stay with you." She tried to swallow. "Which way?"

"Over there." Carter pointed. "At the base of that hill."

This far into the forest, the trees were wider, taller and grew closer together. Tendrils of fog rose from the wet ground, making it impossible to see much beyond where they stood.

They walked to the spot Carter indicated. Two furrows were dug in the soft ground. Fiona turned a slow circle. "The trail ends here."

Carter nodded but said nothing.

Fiona began to shiver. Was it her nerves or had the temperature actually dropped?

"You feel that?" Carter asked, his breath a frozen cloud.

Gooseflesh covered her arms. "It's freezing." What in the hell?

"C'mon. At the top of the hill, we'll get a better view."

They climbed the rise. The opposite slope ended at a clearing. A jagged mountain rose on the other side of the field. A waterfall snaked down the rocky face. Water poured over the mouth of a cave, before emptying into a stream.

Fiona recognized the glade at once. It was the same place where Fiona and Carter had kissed all those years ago. She glanced at Carter. Would being back in the same place release any of his hidden memories? If they came to the surface, what would she say? What would she do?

His tanned complexion was pale. His eyes were narrowed, and his mouth was pressed into a thin and colorless line. She followed his gaze.

On the opposite side of the stream, right at the mouth of the cave, lay a body—bloody and broken. For a moment, she didn't trust her eyes. Then, she knew what she saw was real. Her heart ceased to beat, and she choked back a sob. Even from where she stood, Fiona recognized the person.

It was Dominic.

Chapter 3

The need to tend to the injured man felt like a magnetic pulling from the middle of Carter's chest—but a thousand times stronger. Running to the edge of the stream, he took a knee and examined the body from a distance. The older man's eyes stared at nothing. His mouth gaped, caught in the middle of a horrified scream—probably the one they'd heard in town. His skin was dry and the color of used paste. The neck was a mangled mess of blood, tissue, and gore. The man didn't move—or breathe. In his professional opinion, Dominic was dead. Then again, he'd seen people survive lots of traumas in his life and he needed to make certain.

"Dominic has to be examined."

"I'm coming with you." Fiona had come down from the hilltop and stood at his side.

He gave a terse nod. Yet, there were issues beyond the body and what had caused Dominic's death. First, they had to cross the stream.

The water wasn't deep, but the current was fast—thanks to the storm. A flat rock sat midway between the two banks. Carter took a giant step onto the rock. Icy water rushed over his shoes, leaving his feet numb from the unexpected cold.

Thankfully, the rain had stopped. Yet, the air was chilled, and Carter wished that he would have thought to bring a coat with him.

He held out a palm to Fiona. "Give me your hand."

They touched and his flesh warmed. He pulled her onto the stone. There was barely any room for one person, let alone two. Her breasts pressed against his chest. Her hip was next to his thigh. It was hard to hold onto Fiona and not notice that she was wholly woman. The gleam of her hair. The curve of her bottom lip. The softness of her skin. She smelled of spice, with undertones of vanilla. Standing in the middle of the stream, with Fiona in his arms he had to admit that everything seemed, well—familiar.

Which meant what? Was he now in some kind of crazy déjà vu? Or was it more complicated? Had Carter actually been in this glade before? Then again, did any of it matter—especially since someone needed his care.

"I'll keep you steady." Carter held tight to Fiona's hand as they maneuvered around the stone. "You jump."

She squeezed his hand once and then leapt to the opposite bank. Carter immediately followed.

He approached the body. There wasn't enough neck left to check for a pulse. He grabbed the man's wrist. Nothing. Yet, there was more. Dominic's veins had collapsed.

But how?

"Oh, Dominic." Fiona knelt at the man's side and stroked a strand of hair from his forehead. Anguish evident in each word, she asked, "What happened to you?"

What happened, indeed? Carter started to catalogue what he saw. "He was attacked by some kind of animal." He pointed to the scratches on the face. "Maybe a mountain lion. Or a wolf." Carter knelt to get a closer look at the wound. Certainly, the man's neck had been ripped open by sharp teeth, but... He pointed to two holes under the chin. "It looks like these are puncture marks on his jugular vein." Carter continued, not believing what he was saying. "It looks like Dominic's been drained of all his blood."

"What are you saying?" Fiona stepped closer.

"I don't know how this could've happened. Medically, it's impossible." A scraping sound, like fingernails on a chalkboard, came from inside the cave. Carter stood. "Who's there?"

There was another sound, a rustling, louder this time.

Staring into the mouth of the cave, Carter tried to make out shape or a form. There was nothing to see beyond the darkness. Nothing to hear beyond the rushing stream.

"Hello?"

"Hello?" The voice was raspy and crackled, like dried leaves.

"Are you hurt? Do you need help?"

"Hurt." The voice repeated. "Help."

"Who's there?" Fiona asked, moving to Carter's side.

The voice answered. "Balan. Balan. Balan."

Wide-eyed, Fiona looked at Carter. She made no comment, but he could guess what she was thinking. How in the hell did someone—anyone—around here know his name?

Stepping forward, spray from the waterfall further dampened Carter's clothes. Daylight illuminated the mouth of the cave, before being swallowed by the yawning darkness.

"Are you hurt?" he asked, again. "Do you need

help? Can you come to me?"

Carter listened, trying to hear the voice that called his name. It had gone silent.

The situation was a little too close to what had happened to Carter only a few months ago in the Hindu Kish. Then again, he wasn't in a combat zone. There were no enemies lying in wait. Shaking off the memories, he turned to Fiona. "Whoever's in there is hurt and might not be ambulatory. I need to help. You wait here."

"No way," said Fiona. Had she spoken a little too quickly and maybe with a bit more force than necessary? Was there something about the woods that frightened Fiona? Should Carter be scared, too? Before he could ask, she spoke again—her tone was softer this time. "Besides, what if you need help carrying someone out?"

Carter didn't have a chance to argue. Fiona had already stepped inside the cave. He hated caves but Carter would be damned before he let Fiona take point on the search. And then, he wondered why. Certainly, she was capable. Was it all machismo on his end? Or did he really want to protect Fiona?

Clad in all black, her silhouette blended with the shadows. The fiery red of her hair was the only thing that Carter could see. Jogging to catch up, he reached for her hand and pulled Fiona to a stop. Her skin was soft and warm. Her touch left his heart racing. "I'll go first."

The cave was dank and dark. The continual drip, drip, drip of water sounded in the distance. They walked on, the sunlight barely reaching where they stood. But there was more to the cave than the cold and the water. There was a miasma of scents that turned his stomach. Carter tried to place the smell. It was somehow bitter and yet had the sickly-sweet stench of refuse and decay. "Smell that?" he asked.

"Yuck. I do," said Fiona. She was little more than a shadow in the darkness as her hand slipped from his. She covered her nose with her palm.

"What is it? Is there a sewer line down here?"

"I don't know. It smells like." She paused, as if searching for the right word. "Evil."

Carter's pulse began to race a minute before the blackness became total. With a jolt, it all came back to him.

For the span of a single heartbeat, he was 13 again. He stood in the glade and held a girl's hand. The dying light of day shimmered on the creek, turning the water to molten gold. Carter pulled the girl to him, pressing his lips against hers. The sun slipped below the horizon and a shadow took form, becoming a man with red eyes.

A cold breeze blew on the back of Carter's neck, bring him back to the cave. The flash of memory left him with more questions than answers. Yet, he knew one thing for certain—there was something about the cave. What's more, Fiona had been right about this place.

It was evil.

****

Fiona stopped and an icy shiver ran down her spine. The stench of fetid breath surrounded her. She was lost on an endless ocean of darkness. She could feel a set of eyes on her, staring at the base of her neck—the exact place where her pulse fluttered. Then again, that wasn't possible, right?

"Carter," she whispered, her voice booming in the stillness. "Where are you?"

There was no answer.

45

Was she all alone?

Had she wandered away from Carter? In the darkness, it was impossible to tell where she was. Or where Carter had gone. She had no idea which way would take her out of the cave. One wrong turn and she'd be lost forever.

The whisper of a breath brushed her cheek, and her blood turned cold.

Clenching her hands into fists, Fiona forced her arms to her sides. She dared not reach out, fearful of what she might touch—or what might touch her. Her heartbeat thundered, her pulse echoing in her ears. Holding her breath, she listened.

Was that the crunch of a footfall on loose stone?

The brushing of a sleeve on the damp wall?

The temperature dropped and Fiona began to shiver. Her jaw trembled and she ground her teeth together. She had to get out of the cave.

But how?

Think, Fiona.

She drew a breath and exhaled. In her mind's eye, she saw a bright ball of light. It was an easy spell, one that she'd done since childhood. Lifting her hands, she held her palms toward each other. She pressed them closer, waiting for the resistance of collected power. There was none.

"You?" The inner voice chastised. *"You're the Daughter of the Moon. You're supposed to have power that others do not. What's wrong with you?"*

Her mouth went dry. Without a connection to her magic, she was doomed to die in the darkness.

Fear, a hulking shadow, perched on her shoulder. It weighed her down and left her weary. She whispered, "I cannot let fear or doubt be in control. I am the light."

She lifted her hands again. Fiona felt power swirling in her chest. Her heart pounded painfully against her ribs. Her head ached. A cold sweat dampened her brow. Despite it all, she imagined the tendril of energy stretching down her arms and exploding from her fingertips.

A flame sprang to life between her hands. It flickered and grew.

There was a scuttling noise behind her. She turned, holding out the flame of a single candle. A heap of dull cloth hung on the wall. Then it moved. Turned. The figure was tall—well over 7'. The face was gray. The eyes were red.

Pulse racing, she stepped backward, trying to escape. But go where? She was lost. Trapped. Her skull cracked against the rock wall, filling her head with a white bolt of pain. Her vision grew fuzzy and the flame in her hand dimmed to a tiny spark.

The man with red eyes hissed, exposing a mouthful of sharp and jagged teeth.

What was that? Was it really a vampire? Since adolescence, Fiona had been told that all the vampires were dead.

The creature lunged forward. She lifted her arm, to block the attack. The light in her hand blazed bright. The vampire shrieked, as its red eyes turned black as coal.

In that moment, there was something familiar about the beast.

"Fiona, run!" Carter stood at the opposite side of the chamber.

She sprinted toward him. Her heart pounded against her chest. Her feet slapped the stone floor, the sounds louder than gunshot. Glancing once over her shoulder, she saw the vampire stumble further into the cave, before being swallowed by the darkness.

Beyond Carter, she could see a sliver of white. It was the actual light at the end of the tunnel. Racing to meet her, he grabbed her hand.

"Come on," Carter said, pulling her toward the mouth of the cave.

Her side ached and chest burned. She didn't care and forced her legs to move faster. She raced into the daylight and drew in a shaking breath. "What the hell is that?"

"I saw…" she began. Yet, what had she seen? "He's like…" She shook her head. "He's horrible, like something straight out of a nightmare. I don't think it'll follow us, though. It seems to be afraid of light."

Then she realized her mistake.

Was Carter worried about the creature in the cave? Sure. Yet his gaze was trained on Fiona's out-stretched hand and the ball of fire she held.

"What's that?" he asked again, pointing at her palm.

Fiona knew there was no way she could explain what had just happened without exposing the truth about Ancient Oaks. Closing her palm, she extinguished the flames.

****

Carter stared at Fiona's closed hand. Smoke wafted from between her fingers. He knew what he'd seen—she'd created a sphere of flames in her palm. His brain raced for a logical explanation as his stomach dropped to his shoes.

Did she use lighter fluid—a kind of trick performed all the time? If so, where had she hidden the accelerant or matches.

Even if he could answer that question, there were others he could not. The body of Dominic, lay near where they stood. He'd been drained of his blood—but by what? Then there was the final mystery. What the hell had been in that cavern?

Carter had no idea what was happening. He'd been wrong to come searching for Ancient Oaks. He never should've tried to dig up the past.

There was more though. The sour taste of panic coated his tongue. Why had he gone into a cave—the place where Carter's worst nightmares came true?

Well, the sooner he could get away, the better.

Yet, he couldn't help but ask, "Are you…" No, he couldn't just blurt out what he was thinking, fearing. Working his jaw back and forth, he started over. "How are you? Are you hurt?"

Wiping her palm on the seat of her pants, she shrugged. "I'm fine, getting lost in the cave gave me a start."

So, she wasn't going to mention the flames in her hand or the creature in the cave? Then again, the evasive answer placed Carter at a crossroads of sorts. If he wanted, he could accept her response at face value. That path was clear. First, he and Fiona would return to town and report that they'd found Dominic's body. Carter could honestly say that the cause of death was blood loss from what appeared to be an animal attack. Then, Carter would get in his car and drive back to base, never to think of this day again.

Or he could press Fiona for her candor. Afterall, he had come to Ancient Oaks for answers. Yet, the path that led to the truth was murky and much more dangerous than the safety of ignorance.

He wanted to choose ignorance but couldn't. "What's going on?" he asked. "There's a lot about Ancient Oaks that you aren't saying."

"I don't know what you want me to tell you."

"The flame in your hand. The creature in the cave. You have to tell me, what's going on?"

Standing taller, she squared her shoulders. "Nothing's going on."

If Fiona wasn't going to level with him, so be it. All the same, as a doctor, he had a duty to perform. He had to call someone and report that Dominic had been attacked and was now deceased. Pulling the cellphone from the pocket of his jeans, he dialed Emergency Services. The line was silent. He glanced at the screen. There were no bars.

Gripping the phone tighter, Carter allowed his anger to flare. "What's the matter with this place? You don't even have a damned cellphone tower nearby. That's not normal."

"Normal? Is that what makes someone normal? A cellphone."

"Of course, not. It's just that cellular communication is a way of life."

"Not in Ancient Oaks."

"How do you communicate, then?"

She glanced at him. Their gazes met and held. Fiona looked at the ground. "We have our ways."

A single word filled his mouth. It was crazy, but somehow, he knew it was true. "Magic," he whispered.

She said nothing.

"It's magic," he repeated, his voice louder this time.

Folding her arms across her chest, Fiona looked

back at the cave. "In Ancient Oaks, we work hard to live apart from the rest of the world. What do you think would happen if mortals found out about a town filled with folks who have magical abilities?" She added quickly, "And I'm not saying that Ancient Oaks is a place like that."

Carter's mind filled with images of government labs and painful testing. "Your secrets are safe with me."

"Thank you," she said, her voice low in the quiet woods. "But we have bigger problems." She cast her gaze at Dominic's body. "That thing in the cave did this to him."

It was neither a question, nor a statement. Yet, he nodded. "I think so." The pull to get in his car and leave town was strong. Still, he couldn't just abandon Fiona. Planning as he spoke, Carter said, "I'll get you back to the bookstore and then I have to go."

"Go?" she echoed.

"I need to get back to base." It was an excuse and they both knew it. "Rachel can take care of the body." Exhaling, he started over. "Ancient Oaks isn't my town. I'm not sure why my grandfather came here all those years ago, but we aren't the magical type. Science. Medicine. That's what I believe in. This." He waved his hand, taking in Fiona, the cave, the body, the woods. "None of this belongs to me."

"You sure about that?" Fiona jumped to the stone in the middle of the stream before springing to the opposite bank.

"Am I sure about what?" Carter ran through the water, not bothering with the rock.

Glancing over her shoulder, her gaze met Carter's. "Are you sure that none of this belongs to you?"

He knew what she was asking. He'd come here looking for information about his grandfather. So far, he didn't have any answers—only more questions. He watched her climb the hill. Sunlight had broken through the dark clouds. A beam shone down, turning her hair into a coppery halo. The sense of being at a crossroads was stronger now and he knew that he needed to choose.

Yet, which path? Did he pick order? Or the chaos that came from knowing the truth?

Then again, he really didn't need to make a decision. There was really only one thing for Carter to do.

With a muttered curse, he hustled up the hill. At the top, he reached for Fiona's wrist and pulled her to a stop. "Listen, my grandfather brought me here thirty years ago for a reason. I want to know everything I can about him and about what happened." He paused, knowing what he was about to say was crazy. Then again, everything about today had been crazy already. He started walking. "Something in this town caused his death. I don't have proof, but I can feel it in my bones." Feelings in bones? Is that all the evidence he had? He continued. "I've been having these dreams since coming back stateside." Dreams? What was wrong with Carter. He needed proof, right? He tried one last time. "I owe it to Grandfather Balan—and to myself—to find out what happened."

"I'll be honest, I don't know what happened to your grandfather." Fiona's tucked her hands inside her sleeves as she walked. She continued, "But I can help you learn more of your families' history and who you really are."

"I know exactly who I am." He'd spoken with a sharper tone than he'd intended. Moderating his words, he continued. "I'm a respected doctor. A soldier. A loving son. A loyal friend." He stood at the top of the stairs and looked down on Ancient Oaks. Sure, he'd been standing on Main Street an hour ago. In sixty minutes, nothing had changed and yet, everything was different.

"Come with me" Fiona started to jog down the stone stairs.

Carter followed.

On the sidewalk, she continued. "We'll call the police from my shop and then there's something I want to show you." Fiona led the way back to the bookstore. A CLOSED sign hung in the window. "I guess Lana got tired of waiting." Still, the door was unlocked, and she pulled it open.

Carter stepped inside. The bookstore was exactly the same. Tables piled with books filled the room. Shelves, from floor to ceiling, were filled with volumes. In the corner, sat a round table next to a tea caddy. Mind wandering, his thoughts returned to this same place, yet the day came from decades before.

"This is my grandson, Carter," Grandfather Balan had said, while introducing Carter to the owner of the shop, a woman with dark-rimmed glasses and short red hair. "Carter's a Balan, through and through."

His chest swelled with satisfaction at his grandfather's words and the pride in his tone. Grandfather Balan dropped his hand on Carter's thin shoulder, the gesture was meant for comrades or colleagues, and not grandfather and grandson.

"You're a handsome lad, aren't you? Let me get you a glass of lemonade," said the woman, ushering him to the table by the door. "You can browse while your grandfather meets with us all."

Several people had been milling about the store. Standing in groups of two or three, they spoke in hushed tones. Had Carter overheard any of what had been said? All these years later, he couldn't recall.

Then, the bookshelf at the back of the store opened. Beyond was a small room with teal wallpaper. Carter, a cold glass of lemonade half-way to his mouth, gaped. One by one, the people filed into the space. Carter heard his grandfather's deep voice. "There's one in the woods? Are you sure?" And then, the door closed.

Wiping a hand down his face, Carter gazed out of the book shop's window. Gray clouds once again filled the sky. It seemed that the storm wasn't done with them yet.

"I'll call the police chief," Fiona was saying. Had she been talking all along? "Until then." She walked to a table at the back of the store. Carter followed, noticing the curve of her hips and the sway of her rear. "Here it is," she said, holding out a large book with a leather cover and a brass latch.

Carter read the title out loud. "Diary of a Vampire Hunter, by Rupert Balan." He looked at Fiona. "Are you kidding me? You think that my grandfather was a vampire hunter?"

"You want to learn more about your grandfather. More than that, you saw what I did in that cave. You know what happened to Dominic." She lifted her chin toward the book. "You've been given plenty of evidence but, you have to ask yourself a question. Are you ready to believe?"

Chapter 4

Standing behind the counter, Fiona lifted the phone from the cradle and dialed a number she knew by heart. It was answered on the first ring.

"This is Porter."

"Porter, it's Fiona. I'm at the bookstore with Rupert Balan's grandson. There's been an incident with Dominic." Everything that happened in the woods was still so unbelievable. She glanced toward the table by the door. Carter sat in one of the chairs. The book, written by his grandfather, lay open on his lap. Muted light reflected off the page until it looked as if the book itself glowed.

Carter, brows drawn together, read. He might have asked for the truth, but Fiona imagined that he was currently at war with himself. His mind was telling him one thing, and his heart another.

What would he decide? Fiona had no way of guessing.

"An incident?" Porter echoed Fiona's words. "What happened."

"First." She paused and drew in a shaking breath. There was no way to confront the ugly situation other than with the truth. "Dominic's dead. Balan's a physician and examined the body. It looks like he was attacked by some kind of animal."

"An animal?" Even over the phone, she could hear

the scratching of a pencil on paper as Porter took notes. "What kind of animal?"

"There's more, Porter. We saw a creature in the cave. I think it was responsible for the death."

"Creature?" The sounds of writing stopped. "What's that supposed to mean."

What was she supposed to say? That there's a vampire hiding in the woods? Even though it was what Fiona knew to be true, she couldn't bring herself to say the words—at least, not yet. "I'll explain once you get here. But hurry."

He cursed. "I can't believe that you, of all people, went into the woods. What aren't you telling me?"

"A lot. Just get here as soon as you can. And Porter." She gripped the phone tighter. "Bring the rest of the council—Tad and Rachel. This effects everyone in town."

"I'm on my way," Porter said, ending the call.

She placed the phone back on the cradle. "The police chief is on his way."

Carter nodded slowly, his eyes still on the page. Sure, he'd overheard what she said to Porter, yet there were obviously other things on his mind. Waving his hand toward the book, he leaned back in the chair. "I believe that my grandfather wrote these words. As I read, I can hear his voice in my mind but…" He shook his head.

"But?" she coaxed.

Looking up, he met Fiona's gaze. She tried to ignore the fluttering in her middle—especially since she could guess at what he was about to say next.

"I don't believe a word of it. I mean, look at the list of chapters. *The Vampire Plague of China and Europe.*

56

The Balan Family from Romania and Beyond. And my personal favorite, *Vampires and Vampire Hunting.* Honestly, this reads like fiction." He set the book on the table.

She shrugged and moved to the front window. Maybe it was better if Carter didn't think that any of this was real. In the end, it'd be easier to wipe away his memories for a second time.

Cursing softly, Carter shook his head. "I can't believe I'm about to say this, but Fiona—tell me everything."

Swallowing, Fiona wondered where she should start. Then again, didn't every good story start at the beginning?

"I'm sure you know that the Balan family comes from Bucharest." Leaning a shoulder on the front window, she watched Carter as she spoke.

Carter nodded. "My grandfather was born there. As a child, he emigrated to New York City. Attended NYU. After, he worked his whole life as an architect, specializing in building restoration."

"Your grandfather needed to get into historic places. It's the only way he could search for relics. Clues."

"You're saying that his job was a sham?"

Had his grandfather's job been a ruse? She said, "As far as I know, your grandfather really was an architect and he really worked to preserve historic sites. It's just he was looking for more than cracks in the foundation."

Shaking his head, Carter turned his gaze to the book. "How did my family get started as vampire hunters—if that's even true."

Ah, now there was a question Fiona could answer. She moved to where Carter sat and dropped into the chair opposite. The book sat on the table between them. She found the right page and read out loud. "The Balan Clan has been vampire hunters for centuries." She added her own understanding. "Sure, there's training involved, but a lot of the abilities are innate. Biological, almost."

"Biological," he echoed, pinning her in place with his dark stare. "How?"

"Well." Heat gathered in Fiona's middle and left her flushed. Was it the way he looked at her? Or was it because of what she had next to say? "It's believed that the Balan family originated when a vampire mated with a mortal. This mixing of bloodlines has bestowed certain powers on the Balan's."

"Whoa, whoa, whoa." Carter held up his hands. "You're saying that I'm part vampire?"

She began, "It was generations back, but it's common lore."

"It's bullshit," he interrupted.

"You wanted the truth, Carter. But you have to be willing to accept it." She reached for his wrist. Her fingers touched his flesh, and a tingling began in her palm. She let her hand slip away. "It looks like your grandfather wrote down everything about his life. What else do you want to know?"

"The creature in the cave? What was that?"

Shaking her head, Fiona said, "Honestly, I don't know. I've never seen anything like it."

"Vampire?" he asked, giving voice to her fear.

"Maybe. I've never seen a vampire before. Nobody has. Most people who do, don't survive."

"So, they're only a problem for the magical world?"

Oh, good. Another question Fiona could answer. Rising to her feet, she searched the shelves. *The Great*

Vampire Outbreak. "This is the one." After removing the book, she returned to the table and sat. "The last vampire plague started an Asia. Middle of the nineteenth century. Hundreds of thousands of people died."

Carter stared at her and lifted his brows. "I wasn't a history major, but I did go to med school. I'd recall the class about a bunch of vampires killing over a hundred-thousand people."

"That's because the mortals only saw what they wanted to see. A disease."

"Are you trying to say that the bubonic plague in eighteen fifty-five was caused by vampires?"

"See here." Turning the book toward Carter, she pointed to a passage.

He read out loud. "Over one-hundred vampires descended on the Yunnan province, infecting thousands more. The army of undead spread throughout China and moved into the rest of Asia before facing any resistance. A band of vampire hunters, led by Romanian scholar Florin Balan…"

"That's your great-great-grandfather," Fiona added, when Carter's words trailed off.

He closed the book. "I know what I saw in the cave. The creature. You, creating fire from nothing. But I'll be honest, I'm having a hard time believing that any of this is true."

She wasn't surprised. Mortals lived in a world where magic was dismissed, feared, reviled. Disbelief was their single greatest defense.

He continued, "None of this can be real. It's not scientifically possible."

"Should it be possible to put a man on the moon? Or fly in an airplane?"

"That's physics." Carter slid the book back onto the shelf. "I can't see physics, but I understand it's laws—or some of them, at least. I've never seen anything in the natural world like what I saw today."

"You've never seen air," Fiona countered. "Yet, you breathe."

"Point made." He paused. "Can I ask you a question?"

"Sure."

"Exactly how do you create fire with your hands?"

There was no denying the truth. "Magic."

"Do you learn your magic? Or is it something you're born with?"

"Mortals who work hard can learn how to harness magic, sure," she said. "I happen to have been born into a family of witches. For me, magic is hereditary." *Or rather, was.*

"Your friend, the blonde with all the body glitter? Is she a witch, too?"

"Lana? She's a fairy—born that way. And it's not body glitter. It's her shimmer."

"What can she do?"

"She makes a really good almond cake," said Fiona. "Plus, she can fly."

"No freaking way. So, the tatts on her back aren't tatts."

"Those are wings but tucked in tight."

"Rachel? Tad? Dominic?"

"Witch. Warlock. Fairy."

Before Carter could ask another question, the door opened. Porter—the police chief—stepped into the shop. Porter was tall, almost 6 ½ feet. He was muscular, with powerful arms and broad shoulders. His dark hair was thick, and the ends skimmed the top of his uniform's shirt. A silver badge, affixed to his breast pocket, read *Ancient Oaks Police Department*. Despite the cloudy sky, he wore a pair of sunglasses. Removing the shades, he hooked them into the neck of his uniform shirt.

"I called Rachel," he said by way of greeting. "She was with Lana. They're on the way."

"And Tad?" Fiona asked.

"He didn't answer, but Rachel's stopping by his house. She'll bring him with her."

Removing a small notepad from the pocket of his uniform shirt, Porter hitched his chin toward Carter. "You Balan's grandson? I heard you're a doctor. That true?"

Carter nodded. "I am both Rupert Balan's grandson and a physician."

Porter huffed. "I'd have pegged you for a military man. You have that look."

"So, I've heard," said Carter. "You'd be right about my military service, as well. Major Carter Balan, M.D."

Porter nodded slowly. "An Army Doc. Impressive. Well, impressive for one of your kind. Tell me what happened."

Carter decided not to be offended by the police officer's comment. "We were standing by my car when we heard a scream. It sounded like it came from the woods. Fiona and I went to investigate. Just over the tree line, we found a drag marks in the leaves. A puddle of blood. There was also a bloody handprint on a tree trunk."

"We found Dominic near the waterfall," Fiona said, picking up the story where Carter left off.

"I know the place," said Porter.

Of course, he did. Porter knew every inch of the forest. As kids, they'd played in the woods all of the time. It was before Fiona decided that she hated the out of doors.

Pushing all her childhood memories aside, she focused only on today. "Dominic was a mess." Her eyes burned and her chest ached with the loss of her friend. "His neck had been ripped open."

"There were puncture marks." Carter pointed to the underside of his chin. "His veins were empty, too."

"Empty?"

"It was like, well." Carter exhaled. "His blood had been consumed."

Porter grimaced. "You're a doctor. Is that possible?"

"Maybe, but not by any animal I've ever encountered."

"Oh?" Porter looked at Fiona from the side of his eye. She could see the question in his glance. *What does this guy know?*

There was no point in hiding what she'd done. "We saw a creature—almost human—in the cave. I was able to scare it away by conjuring a ball of flames." She continued. "Carter saw what he saw. It wasn't my plan, but I told him the truth about everything."

"Everything?" Porter snarled.

Fiona didn't have time to feel guilty. Lifting her chin, she said, "He's Rupert Balan's grandson. This world is his as much as it's ours."

"He's lived as a mortal his entire life and you know that mortals can't be trusted."

"Listen." Carter held up his hands in surrender. "I agree with you both. I am a mortal. I am also Rupert's grandson. I'll take all of your secrets with me to the grave, but this isn't my world." He hooked a thumb toward the door. "In fact, if you don't need anything more from me, I should go."

Fiona knew that Carter was right, he really should leave town. Until they knew more about the creature in the cave, Ancient Oaks wasn't safe for anyone—especially a mortal with no magical skills.

Then again, it was also true that she didn't want Carter to leave. Before she could decide what to say, the door burst open. The bells above the door jangled, dancing wildly on the hook.

Rachel, white-faced and sweating, entered the store. Lana was right behind. She was pale and her hands shook.

"What's the matter?" Porter asked, his brown eyes turning amber.

"It's Tad," Rachel croaked. "He's not home. I looked through the window. His house is a wreck. I think." She drew in a shaking breath. "I think he's been taken."

****

Tad, the mayor of Ancient Oaks, lived on the outskirts of town. Everyone—Carter included—piled into the police chief's SUV for the short drive. Parking on the side of the road, Porter turned off the auto's engine. "Here we are."

From the passenger seat, Carter opened the door and stepped from the vehicle. Tad's home—a single-level stone house, better suited for a fairytale than the modern world, was surrounded by a stone fence and an over-grown lawn. Two pumpkins, already carved into jack-o-lanterns, smiled and sat on the stoop. A tree stood in the middle of the yard; the bare branches reached for the sky.

The back of the property ended at the woods.

Rachel and Lana slipped out of the backseat. Both women wore similar expressions, with their faces pale and brows drawn together. He'd seen the look more than once. The women were anxious, or at least worried. Fiona was the last to exit the vehicle. His gaze met hers for a single second. Then, she looked away. What was she thinking? Did she see Carter as an intruder? Or was she happy that he had come along?

In the bookstore, nothing had been said to the other women about Carter and Fiona's experience in the woods. While everyone stood outside the gate, Porter took a moment to brief Lana and Rachel. "You both know Carter Balan, Rupert's grandson," he began. "Seems he and Fiona found Dominic's body near the waterfall. They also saw a creature in the cave—something dark and evil. What's worse, Fiona decided to tell Carter everything about Ancient Oaks."

"Everything?" Lana squeaked.

"Not everything," Fiona corrected. "Just as much as he needed to know."

"Which is pretty much everything," Porter added.

Rachel stepped forward and placed her palm on Carter's breastbone. The older woman's hand was strong and warm. The flesh beneath her palm tingled. What was causing the sensation? Was it magic? Before he could ask, Rachel spoke. "He has the heart of a Balan. The Daughter of the Moon took him into her confidence. What's more, I believe he's one of the few mortals who will be faithful to our secrets."

Daughter of the Moon? He guessed that she meant Fiona, but why the title?

"Fine, then," Porter growled. The question of

whether Carter should be trusted—or not—seemed to have been answered. Then, just as quickly, the big guy moved on to the next problem. "Let's see what's going on with Tad."

After pushing open a gate, the cop strode up the walk. Knocking on the door with the side of his fist, Porter said, "Tad. It's me. Open up."

There was no answer from inside the house. In fact, there was no noise—save for a hawk screeching in the distance.

"Let's go see what's going on." Lana held open the gate.

"Good idea," said Rachel, as Fiona stepped through.

Without comment, Carter followed. Drawing near to the front window, his steps faltered. The curtains were opened, giving him a clear view into the house. From the sofa, recliner, and a glass-top coffee table, he guessed that he was looking at a typical living room.

Then again, there was nothing typical about what he saw.

The chair lay on its side. A sofa cushion was torn, and the table was shattered into a thousand pieces.

"Looks like there's been a hell of a struggle," Carter said, walking across the lawn to get a better look at the destruction.

Porter banged on the door with enough force to rattle the frame. "Tad, you in there?"

"What if he's hurt and can't answer?" Lana asked.

It was exactly what Carter feared. Though there was more that bothered him. "I don't like that this house is so close to the woods. From what I can tell, the creature is bothered by light." He still wasn't ready to name the beast in the cave as a vampire. "But somehow it's able to move through the woods."

"At least if it's cloudy," Fiona added.

She was right. The sun had been behind the clouds when they heard the screams. They day was still overcast. Which meant, what? That the creature from the cave could be watching them—even now?

"Tad, I'm coming in." Pushing the door open, the big guy gagged. Eyes watering, Porter looked at Carter. "What the hell is that stink?"

Even from several yards away, Carter could smell the scents of decay, rot, and well, evil. "I'm not exactly sure where it comes from—but the cave smelled the same way."

The cop wore an automatic pistol in a holster at his side. He unsnapped the latch and stepped into the house. "Jeeze Doc, will you take a look at this kitchen? Every utensil must've been dumped."

Carter followed. The living room filled the front of the house. A short hallway ran to the left and at the back, a narrow doorway led to the kitchen. Carter peered into the room. Knives, forks, and spoons were scattered all over the floor. Cups and glasses were broken into pieces. A butcher knife was lodged into the wall.

Rachel stood behind Carter. The older woman sucked in a breath. "I saw the living room from the lawn—that's when I got worried. But this, well, something definitely happened." She closed her eyes and held out her hands. "I can sense chaos and anger."

"Not to be disrespectful, Rachel," said Porter. "But nobody needs a spell to see the chaos and anger. Both are kind of obvious."

"What happened in here?" Lana asked. She stood just inside the living room. Fiona waited on the threshold. The fairy scanned the room, her eyes wide. "Where's Tad?"

Porter huffed, his nostrils flaring. "Did I invite any of you inside? I'm considering this a crime scene and I don't want anything to get contaminated. All of you." He pointed to the door. "Go."

"We want to help," said Fiona. "You can't just send us away."

"You want to help? Go and talk to everyone in town. Figure out who saw Tad last."

"Anything else?" Lana asked.

"Yeah, nobody's allowed to go into the forest. That's a police order. Spread the word."

Carter turned for the door. Maybe now was the time for him to leave Ancient Oaks. The creature in the cave definitely had an aversion to light. It meant that he didn't want to be anywhere near Ancient Oaks after it got dark.

"Not you, Doc," said the cop. Carter froze, mid-stride. "I need a second set of eyes here. Before now, I would've called Tad. You see why that can't happen today."

Always being ready to assist was part of Carter's DNA, which meant he was stuck helping. "You've got me as long as you need me." Carter glanced out the window. Lana and Fiona stood on the lawn. Rachel was at the door.

"Meet us back at the bookstore," said the older witch. "If we find Tad before then, we'll send word." Then she left.

Lana and Rachel walked down the path, yet Fiona lingered. Carter's gaze met hers. Staring into her blue eyes felt like diving into warm ocean waters—and what's more, he never wanted to come up for air. For the first time in his life, Carter felt the blood actually pump through his veins. It was as if all the days before today, he hadn't really been alive. Until now, he'd simply existed.

It wasn't just the hunt for whatever they were after, either. It was Fiona. She had awakened something within Carter that he didn't even know had been sleeping.

****

For an hour, Carter helped as the cop search through Tad's house. The Mayor was nowhere to be found. What was worse, there were no clues—other than the stench from the cave—as to what happened. With nothing else to investigate, they left the house and drove back to the bookstore.

Sitting in the passenger seat of Porter's SUV, Carter's mind raced—filled with several questions he wanted to ask.

"So," Carter began, starting with a question that wasn't exactly on his list. "How long have you lived in Ancient Oaks?"

"All my life," said the cop. Turning the steering wheel, he maneuvered the big SUV around a corner and onto Main Street.

"You must know everyone pretty well."

"It's a small town. You know how it goes. There are no secrets."

Carter chuckled. He'd spent his entire life near big cities and on military installations. "I know next to nothing about small towns." He paused. "I was just wondering if you knew of anyone who might want to hurt the mayor."

"Hurt Tad?" he echoed. "Not that I could sniff out. I have to say that your question surprises me."

"How so?"

"I thought for sure you'd want to ask me about Fiona."

Carter glanced out the window. His reflection was superimposed on the glass. Even he could see the longing on his face. "Why would you think that I'd want to know about Fiona?"

"Because you like her. You stink of pheromones."

"That's quite a powerful sense of smell you have." Carter paused. "Or is it some kind of magical ability? Are you a fairy, too?"

Porter parked the SUV next to the curb. Across the street was the bookstore. "Give me a break. Do I look like a fairy to you?"

Carter had only seen two fairies in his life—Dominic and Lana. They were both slightly built, blonde, and somehow golden. Porter was darkly complected, muscled. If Lana were made of air, Porter was made of stone—probably granite.

"To be honest," he said, answering the cop's question. "I'm not sure what they should look like. If I had to guess, then I'd say you're the person who's the opposite of a fairy."

"Damn straight." Porter turned off the ignition and slipped the keys into the breast pocket of his uniform. "Besides, I hate heights. I'd never be able to fly."

"So, what are you? A warlock? That's a male witch, right?"

"It is a male witch, but I'm not one of those either." Opening the door, Porter stepped from the auto. "Me, I'm a werewolf."

Carter's chin went slack. For a moment, he couldn't bring himself to close his mouth. After jumping down to the sidewalk, he slammed the door closed. Sure, he'd never divulge anything about his time in Ancient Oaks—but it didn't mean he wasn't curious.

"A werewolf, huh?" he said, matching his pace to that of the other man. "Were you born that way, or did you get bitten?"

"My family is one of the original to Ancient Oaks, so my pack goes back for generations. Sometimes people get bitten. If the bite is bad enough, they'll change."

In getting answers, Carter only had more questions. Yet, as Porter opened the door to the bookstore, he knew he'd have to wait. Lana, Rachel and Fiona all sat at the round table. They looked up as Porter and Carter crossed the threshold.

Rachel stood. "Did you find any clues at Tad's house? Please tell me that you did."

With a shake of his head, Porter said, "I wish I had better news. The house was a wreck. But aside from everything being broken, there was no evidence that a crime had been committed at all."

"Nothing?" Fiona asked.

"Well." Porter adjusted the firearm he wore at his side. "It smelled like an outdoor toilet in the middle of summer. According to the Doc, it's the same smell from the cave. How'd you all fare? Who saw Tad last?"

"It seems like the last person who talked to Tad was me." Rachel continued, "After we spoke to Fiona and Carter, he left the clinic."

"Did he say where he was going?" Carter asked.

Rachel shook her head. "Home, I guess."

Lana asked, "What do we do now?"

"Well, we can't quit looking for Tad," Fiona added.

"Let's all be smart about this," said Rachel. "It's not

hard to figure out that Tad was taken by whatever's living in the cave."

"And what is it?" Lana asked.

For a beat, nobody spoke. Then Carter said, "It's a vampire."

"My dear," said Rachel. "Vampires have been gone for more than a generation. It can't be a vampire."

"Then what do you call an evil creature, who drinks blood and can't stand direct light?" Carter asked.

"Sounds like a vampire to me," said Porter. "Much as I hate to have one of those undead bastards close to town."

Lana's golden glow took a jaundiced tint. "We can't leave it in the cave and pretend it's not there. Eventually, it will come out and get someone else."

"My number one concern is Tad." Porter continued. "We have to find him and save him."

"He's everyone's concern," said Fiona. "But what do we do now?"

Porter said, "Easy. We go and get him."

The hair on Carter's neck stood on end. For an instant, he was whisked away to a different time and place. There had been a cave in another mountain range and missing troops.

Sure, nobody in the bookstore had asked Carter for his opinion. Yet, what he had to say was pretty damned important. "I don't know that going into the cave is a great plan. Actually, I think it's a really bad idea."

Porter's eyes turned from brown to amber. "How so?"

"You didn't see that creature." He paused. "The vampire is nothing if not deadly."

"Fiona saw him. She said she chased him away with

nothing more than a ball of flames. We take torches. Bright flashlights. Fiona and her magic." Porter counted off the items on his fingers as he spoke. "There's only one way into the cave and one way out, so the vampire can't sneak out through the back. If we go now, we can rescue Tad before nightfall."

"What if he's already dead?" Fiona asked.

"What if he's not?" Porter countered.

"I'd like a little more of a plan," said Fiona. "There's a lot that can go wrong."

Carter agreed but said nothing. True, if he wanted to be part of the rescue team, he could. Then again, he'd already fought in his own war.

In the distance, thunder rolled. It was like an alarm, telling him it was time to leave. "Sounds like more rain's coming. I should go."

Carter didn't wait for a response and walked to the door. He pulled it open as a gust of wind forced the door to close. Fighting against the gale, he opened the door for a second time and quickly stepped onto the street. The door slammed shut behind him. Glancing once more over his shoulder, he looked through the window. Inside, Fiona watched him. Lifting his hand, Carter gave a quick wave. Then, he leaned into the wind and trudged away.

Chapter 5

Fiona stood next to the window and watched Carter walk down the street. Like she'd swallowed glass, her throat was sore. "We really didn't need him to stay," she said, the last word crumbling as she spoke.

"What is it with you and that guy?" Porter asked.

Turning from the window, she looked at her friend. "What is what with who?"

"Him. Carter Balan. You kissed him once when we were all kids and then he left. You were sick with a broken heart for about a week. After that, you refused to go into the woods."

"Carter isn't the reason I don't like the forest." Then again, what was?

Ignoring her, Porter continued, "Now, you're about to cry."

She blinked hard. "I am not."

Porter snorted. "I can smell salt from your tears."

"Do you have to be so blunt about everything?"

"It's part of my charm." Brushing his fingertips toward the door, he said, "Go after him. Say goodbye properly. Then, for the love of all that's good—get him out of your system. I can't have you distracted if we're going to save Tad."

Fiona looked down. "He's not in my system and I won't be distracted."

"We'll be fine, dear." Rachel placed her hand on

Fiona's arm. "You can take a minute."

At least her friend, Lana, would be some kind of support, right? Wrong.

Turning her hand upside down, Lana used two fingers to mime walking.

Fiona had never spent enough time with Carter to create unfinished business. Still, she wanted to see him one more time—even if it would be her last. Without another word, she rushed from the store. Carter was halfway down the block. "Carter!" she called. The wind caught her word and swept it away. She started to run. "Carter, wait."

Glancing over his shoulder he saw Fiona and stopped.

"Don't go," she said, jogging the last few yards. Wind pulled a tendril of hair out of the bun. She wiped it from her face. "Don't go," she said again. "We need your help. You're a vampire hunter."

He shook his head and she stopped speaking. "That's just the thing. I'm not. Maybe my grandfather was, but not my dad. Not me."

"But you are." She stopped before saying anything more. Begging Carter to stay hadn't been a part of her plan. Fiona only came outside to say one final goodbye.

"Here's what I am." Carter stepped forward and raised his voice to be heard over the gusting wind. "I'm a regular guy. I'm not a werewolf. I can't fly. I can't make fire with my hands. If I go with you, I'll be a hindrance to the mission."

"You won't." She moved closer to him.

"Honestly, I will." He placed a hand on her shoulder and squeezed. "I'm not exactly glad that I came looking for Ancient Oaks, but I am happy that I found you."

That was her cue to leave. All she needed to do was to tell Carter that she was happy to have met him, too. Yet, his touch was warm and inviting. She wanted to move closer, not walk away.

A raindrop fell, splashing on Fiona's cheek. Carter wiped it away with his thumb. He cupped her chin with his palm. "You better go inside. Doctor's orders."

"I probably should." She leaned into his touch as another raindrop fell.

"Well, then." He took another step closer—a dare and an invitation all in one.

Did Fiona want to accept? Then again, she could never walk away from this moment. Winding her arms around his neck, Fiona drew Carter to her. He brushed his lips over her mouth.

Rain began to fall.

Carter wrapped his arms around her waist and pulled him to her. She deepened the kiss, not caring about the deluge. As if her blood were electrified, she vibrated from the top of her head to the soles of her feet. She sighed and he slipped his tongue inside her mouth.

The kiss deepened as Carter tasted, touched, explored. Fiona felt as if she were an uncharted land. What was more, she was ready to be claimed and conquered. She traced his chest. The fabric of his shirt was wet, yet his muscles were unmistakable. He gripped her rear, pulling her to him. He was hard and what's more, she wanted him after a single kiss.

No, that's not true. Wanting was a paltry word for Fiona's desire. She needed Carter inside of her like someone dying of thirst needs water to survive. Her heart began to race. Somewhere, in the back of her mind, she heard rushing water and a scream.

Trembling, she pushed away from the embrace.

Rain dripped down her nose. Her clothing was sodden, and her teeth began to chatter. "I should go," she said. This time, she didn't wait for Carter's reply. Turning, Fiona ran down the street as the rain hid the tears that threatened to fall.

****

Carter slid into his car and asked himself a single important question. Was he really going to leave Ancient Oaks—and Fiona—behind? Rain fell, bouncing off the pavement and the sidewalk. His clothes were damp. After starting the engine, he turned on the heater. Hot air blew into the car. Using a vent, he warmed his hands and knew that he'd been honest when he said that he'd be an encumbrance on the rescue operation. He wasn't a magical guy—even if past generations possessed certain skills.

Then again, there were other reasons that kept him out of that cave.

With another curse, he shoved the gearshift into drive and pulled away. The drive back to the main road seemed shorter than the one which took him to town. Within minutes, he nosed his car onto the covered bridge. Roiling water was visible through chinks in the wood.

Moments later, he pulled onto the rural highway. He tried to feel triumphant for having escaped from Ancient Oaks, but his chest was tight. Finding a radio station that played rock-n-roll, Carter turned up the volume and let the music drown his thoughts. After driving four miles, he knew it was a wasted effort.

True, the conflict in the magical town wasn't his. It was also true that a direct assault on the cave by those in

Ancient Oaks would be a disaster. It was just like the time when he was deployed with a combat unit overseas. A local merchant came to the base camp, telling the guards he needed to speak to an American doctor. The doc they found was Carter.

"Many men are wounded. Hurt." The merchant had a single dog tag, taken from the lieutenant in command of a missing platoon. "He gave me this. You must hurry."

"You know the location of these men?" Carter asked.

The man nodded vigorously. "I do. Come. Come."

Sure, English wasn't the man's first language, but he spoke well enough for Carter to understand—and believe every word he'd said. In less than an hour, another platoon left base, with Carter and a full medical team in tow.

There'd been heavy fighting in the area for months. As he thought back to the uneventful hump into the mountains, he realized that the lack of an attack should have been his first clue that something was horribly wrong.

The cave was little more than a slit in the side of a hill. "There." The man pointed. "You'll find them there."

The narrow opening forced Carter and the team to spread out to an indefensible single-file line. That should have been his second clue.

Inside the cave, eight men lay on the stone floor. "Cripes, Major," a Sargent grumbled. "I don't think we have much need of a doc. It's more like a job for a coroner."

The sergeant was right. The men were dead—all accept one. Had everyone died of their injuries while the merchant came for help?

Wild-eyed, the lone survivor waved his arms as Carter approached. He groaned. There was something wrong with the soldier's mouth. Dropping to his knees, he skidded toward the other man. The soldier tried to scream but couldn't. It was then Carter saw and understood. The GI's tongue had been cut out. It was clue number three.

The fourth clue followed in an instant. Carter scanned the cave.

"Where's the local guy?"

"Dunno, Major." A medic knelt next to the corpse of a private, who looked far too young to be in the Army, much less dead.

The soldier without a tongue pushed Carter into the dirt and covered him with his own body. There was a blast of light. Scorching heat. A concussion slammed into Carter's chest.

It was then that Carter understood. It was an ambush—plain and simple. One of the bodies—or hell, maybe it was all of the bodies—had been connected to a trip wire. Once they were moved, a bomb exploded. Outside the cave there were screams of the injured and the constant rat-a-tat-tat of automatic gunfire.

Had it not been for the lone soldier, Carter wouldn't have survived.

Dropping his foot on the break, the car skidded to a stop. Screwing his eyes shut, he saw the carnage. This time, it wasn't the mangled bodies of the soldiers who filled his brain. Now, it was those who he had left behind in Ancient Oaks. Porter, no longer breathing, lay in a heap of blood and fur. Lana, too, was dead. Somewhere in the darkness, Fiona screamed.

Opening his eyes, Carter stared out of the rain-streaked windshield. He had to go back to Ancient Oaks and tell them all what happened in the Hindu Kish. Tad was nothing more than bait, meant to drawn them all into a deadly trap.

Rolling back his shoulders, he turned the car around on the narrow and deserted road. It was four miles to the turn off. In less than ten minutes, he'd be back in town. If he was lucky, they'd listen to his warning.

And then what? For starters, his conscience would be clear.

Did he really need another reason?

Carter slowed his speed to a creep. Bending low, he stared out of the window and looked for the sign. He knew that he was in the right place, but there was nothing beyond a solid wall of trees.

Unless he found his way back to Ancient Oaks, Carter knew that all of them—Porter, Lana, Rachel, and Fiona—would die.

****

In the bookstore, Fiona leaned against the counter. The table near the door was piled high with gear. There was half of a dozen high-powered flashlights. Three torches. A lantern. A spotlight. They also had a flare gun and seven flares. Certainly, they had enough lumens to light up the each and every cavern.

On another table lay a map of the cave system—supplied by Porter. From what Fiona could tell, there were 17 different caverns—and Tad could be in anyone of them.

Beyond gathering the lights and the map, a quick scan of: *A Diary of a Vampire Hunter* had revealed an easy-to-follow tip. The book had suggested that vampire hunting required thick clothing—preferably made from leather. Vampire fangs, so Rupert Balan had written, are much stronger than human teeth. Moreover, if broken they grew back in weeks. Yet, they were teeth, not diamonds, and couldn't cut through tough fabrics.

Everyone gathered—Rachel, Lana, Porter, and Fiona—now wore leather. Fiona had donned a leather duster in chocolate brown. Underneath, she had on a thick wool turtleneck, leather leggings and thigh-high leather boots. Lana's outfit was similar, yet all of her leather was all light blue. If Fiona didn't know better, she'd think that her friend was getting ready for a night out in the mortal world.

Porter wore a motorcycle jacket, gloves, chaps and boots. Rachel had a high-necked leather dress and boots.

"Sunset is two hours," said Porter. "By then, we have to be out of the woods. Got it?"

"Got it."

"Everyone take a flashlight," he said, handing them all around. "Keep the light on at all times even though all we really need is our secret weapon. Fiona."

Her stomach dropped to her shoes. "Me?"

"Of course, it's you." Lana popped the collar of her jacket. "You're the Daughter of the Moon. Besides, you're the one who can conjure fire."

Daughter of the Moon. Ugh. Sometimes, she hated that stupid title, but never more than she did right now. The weight of the whole town rested on her shoulders, and she just wanted…Well, she didn't know what she wanted. Then again, her aspirations didn't matter—not when she needed to be honest.

"What happens if I can't perform any spells?"

"But you can," said Porter.

Fiona chewed on her bottom lip. "You aren't

listening to me, Porter. I. Can't. Control. My. Fire."

"Yes, you can," he said, again. "I've seen you make flames out of nothing dozens of times. Hell, it's probably more like hundreds."

Fiona looked down at the floor. She could feel their eyes on her. *Just be honest,* urged her inner voice. *Just tell them you're a failure.* Each word landed like a punch to the gut, yet the voice continued. *And that you're no Daughter of the Moon.*

Fiona kept her gaze on the floor, all the while knowing what kept her silent. If she weren't the Daughter of the Moon, who would she be? Was there anything about her—beyond the title—that made her special?

"Didn't you make a ball of flames today?" Rachel asked.

"I did. But whatever happened in the cave today was a lucky break."

"You're always so humble, Fiona." Lana patted her shoulder. "But now's not the time."

Fiona wanted to scream. Sure, her friends knew her well. In many ways they knew her better than she knew herself. Yet, this time was different. This time, they were letting their shared history get in the way of what she needed them to hear. The question was—how could she make them understand? She wasn't anybody's secret weapon. In fact, she wasn't going to be much help at all.

****

Carter's jaw was tight, and his eyes felt gritty. He'd driven the same mile-long strip of pavement eleven times. Slowing the car at the exact place where he found the road to Ancient Oaks, he scanned the woods. There was nothing beyond the trees. No sign. No road. Not even the bridge.

"What the hell?" he muttered. Sure, he knew the place was magical. And yeah, he had kind of figured out that magic kept it hidden from the rest of the world. It's just that he never imagined that if he found it once, he wouldn't be able to find it again.

How had it found the road the last time?

Oh, yes. Carter remembered. Pulling to the side of the road, he parked in the same place as before. He'd looked at the map and the picture of his grandfather. Carter repeated the actions. What else?

He'd breathed deeply several times. Inhale. Hold. Exhale. Hold. Then, he'd raced down the road.

Carter maneuvered the car back onto the asphalt and dropped his foot onto the accelerator. The car shot forward, pressing him back into the seat. He glanced out the window. The woods were a multicolored blur.

He slammed on the breaks. The car fishtailed on the wet pavement, and he steered into the skid. Coming to a stop, he glanced in the rearview mirror and smiled. There, where it hadn't been before, stood a sign. Ancient Oaks. Three miles. He backed up and turned down the narrow lane.

After driving less than 100 yards, he stopped. Water lapped at the cut of the bridge. Halfway across, the current ran over the boards. Carter swallowed. Driving across a bridge that was underwater was a special kind of stupid.

He hadn't come all this way to turn back now. Backing up ten yards, he unrolled his window and removed his seatbelt. Cold air poured into the car and the seatbelt sensor pinged a warning. At least if the car got pushed into the creek, he wouldn't be trapped inside.

Revving the engine, he focused on the opposite bank. Pressing his foot on the gas, he shot down the road. His front tires rumbled over the bridge. Water pushed against his car. Carter tightened his grip on the steering wheel to keep the tires straight.

The auto shot off the bridge as if launched by a cannon. Carter slowed and took a deep gulping breath. Sure, getting back to Ancient Oaks had been difficult. But he knew that the struggle was just beginning. More than stopping Fiona—and everyone else—from getting ambushed in the cave, Carter decided to stay in town. This time, he was going to fight the vampire himself.

****

Maybe Fiona's friends were right. Maybe she did still control her powers. After all, she'd used them today. Maybe if she just believed in herself, as she was taught to do all those years ago, then everything would turnout just fine. Yet, while standing at the bottom of the stone staircase and looking into the woods, she knew that nothing about this rescue mission was going to be fine.

Porter stood at her side. "Are you ready?"

She was far from ready. Then again, what more could she say. She inhaled deeply and opened her hands. Could she feel the magic flowing around her fingertips? Or was that simply a breeze?

"I'm ready."

She took one step and looked down the street. In the days and weeks that followed, Fiona could never explain what had caught her attention first. Had it been the far-off revving of an engine? Had she seen the glint of a headlight in the gloomy afternoon? Or had her heart skipped a beat as Carter came closer?

She looked down the street. The multicolored

bunting on the bakery—orange, gold, red—flapped in the gathering storm. Everyone's gaze followed.

"I'll be damned," said Porter. "It's the Doc. He found us again."

Carter stopped the car in the middle of the road. With the engine still running, he opened the door and stepped out. "Thank goodness I found you before it's too late."

"Too late for what?" Lana asked.

"Listen." His breathing was labored, as if he'd just sprinted the three miles from the mortal road and not driven in his car. "You can't go into that cave."

Fiona took a step back. Did he know about her and her waning skills? And if so, how?

Porter held up his big hand. "Hold on one minute, Doc. That creature. The vampire. Whatever it is, it took Tad. You smelled the beast in his house. You said so yourself. We have to save the mayor."

"It's a trap. An ambush. None of you will make it out alive."

"What makes you so certain?" It was Rachel who asked the question.

After drawing a long breath, he rubbed a hand over the back of his neck. "The same thing happened to me in combat. We were told that a missing platoon was injured and recuperating in nearby cave. They needed a doctor, so I went. One of the bodies was boobytrapped." He exhaled and looked away. Fiona's fingertips throbbed with the need to touch Carter, to offer him comfort. Yet, she dared not. "That thing in the cave took Tad so you'd come and get your friend. The vampire knows enough to use your goodness against you."

"How long ago did all of this happen?" Again, it was

Rachel who spoke. "Your time in combat."

"Not long enough." Carter stuffed the tips of his fingers into front pockets of his jeans.

Porter nodded. "I hate to admit it, but the Doc does have a point."

"What're we supposed to do then?" Lana asked.

"That's a good question." Porter folded his arms across his chest. "I hope that the doctor has an answer."

Carter shook his head. "I might've been in the Army, but I sewed people up. I never came up with a strategy or sent them into battle."

"Then I'll ask again," said Lana. "What're we supposed to?"

"I don't know," said Carter. "I don't have a plan."

Fiona stepped forward. "Yet."

Carter drew his brows together. "What?"

"You don't have a plan *yet*." Fiona emphasized the last word.

"I don't have a plan at all. I don't know anything about vampires." Carter sighed and shook his head. "What you need is a vampire hunter, not me."

Rachel said. "All of the vampire hunters are gone. Rupert Balan was the last of his kind."

For the past few minutes, Fiona felt as if she'd been an audience member watching a play. Yet, she now knew her part. "Your grandfather may be dead, but it doesn't mean that his words or wisdom has disappeared." She looked down the street. There, in the middle of the block, sat her store. "We have his book, Carter. You have your innate abilities. There's lots to learn about vampires— and together, we can do it."

"I don't like leaving Tad in the cave," said Porter.

"None of us want to leave Tad," said Fiona. "But

what help are we going to be if we end up dead?"

Porter lifted his big hands in surrender. "You have tonight to find out everything you can and come up with a better plan."

"And what happens if they don't?" Lana asked.

"Then," said Porter. "We won't have any choice. Ambush or not, we'll have to go into the cave."

Chapter 6

Like an ebony cloak had been pulled across the sky, night came to Ancient Oaks. Before nightfall, Porter had collected Dominic's body, so he no longer lay near the cave. Rachel and Lana had alerted everyone in town about the danger lurking in the woods and told them all to stay inside. As far as Fiona could tell—the order had been followed.

Carter and Fiona had returned to the bookstore. Fiona had taken some time to change out of her leather outfit and now wore a cashmere sweater in deep, hunter green along with a pair of fawn swede legging and booties in the same color. True, she was overdressed for a night of looking through books, but for the first time in ages Fiona wanted to look nice.

It wasn't hard for her to figure out why. She hoped to impress Carter Balan.

While in her upstairs apartment, Fiona had made sandwiches. Now, the empty plates sat on the table. Fiona had kicked off her boots, which lie in the middle of the floor.

They'd spent hours learning everything they could about vampires. The list, written on a pad of paper, sat next to the empty plates. Atop the pad, was a pen.

Picking up the paper, Carter scanned the list of verified facts about vampires. He read out loud, "Most vampire attacks are fatal, as the vampire consumes the victim's blood. But, if a vampire merely bites a mortal, then it transfers venom—thus turning the mortal to one of the undead. The antidote for vampire venom is to consume the ashes of a burned vampire," he said.

Fiona added a fact she'd read only moments before. "The ashes have to be mixed with red wine, but true."

"Red wine," he repeated, adding the notation. "Second, vampires cannot enter a dwelling unless invited. Third, sunlight doesn't destroy a vampire—it blinds them."

"Correct." Fiona couldn't help but think about those terrifying moments in the cave as the vampire's eyes changed from glowing red to black. "The effects can last for days, or even weeks. Who knows, if the light were bright enough, the vampire might not be able to see for months. And it's not just sunlight, but any direct and bright light. Electrical light. Even candlelight works, but that's not as strong."

"What about sunglasses? Would a pair of sunglasses offer protection? With them, could a vampire go out during the day?"

It was a reasonable question. "To be honest, I don't know. People, like your forefathers, used to study the undead. But I don't know if anyone thought about sunglasses in the nineteenth century." She paused. "You're starting to think like one of them, you know."

"One of what?" he asked, though she suspected that he knew the answer.

"A vampire hunter. It's in your DNA."

"Vampire hunter." He shrugged. "I'm trying to understand what's going on is all."

"What does your DNA tell you?" She was partly teasing Carter, partly asking a serious question. "Have you learned anything helpful?"

"First, the vampire is an apex predator. Sure, it kills to survive, but there's more." He pointed to the list. "It eats rarely. From this chart, it looks like it can only consume a whole human once a month—and can actually go for years without human blood."

"I guess that's a little bit of good news for Tad. Since the vampire drained all of Dominic's blood, it won't want Tad now. Then again, why take him if not for food?"

"That question actually touches on one of my greatest fears." Carter rubbed the back of his neck. "There's over a dozen times in human history that a single vampire has created a horde. The horde causes massive amounts of death. Even a single vampire can wipe out an entire town."

"Is the vampire trying to create a horde by taking Tad? Or is it picking us off, one by one?"

Shaking his head, Carter said, "I don't know. I guess the best way to deal with the possibilities is to get rid of the creature now."

In a purely academic sense, everything they'd learned was interesting. And, yet they were seeking knowledge to meet an end. "Has anything helped you come up with a plan?"

"The thing about being blinded by light is why they're creatures of the night—although, that's not too hard to figure out. It's also why." He paused before starting again. "After my grandfather died, my parents moved the whole family to Southern California. Even at the time, the move seemed abrupt."

"What are you trying to say?" she asked.

"I'm starting to wonder if my grandfather's death

had something to do with a vampire and his visit to Ancient Oaks." He paused. "Then again, I have bigger problems than what happened thirty years ago."

"It's *we*," she said. "We have bigger problems and." It was her turn to pause. She inhaled. Exhaled. "When all this is over, I'll help you figure out what happened to your grandfather."

He smiled and Fiona's blood filled with fire. "Thanks." He dropped his gaze to the sheet of paper. "Anyway, the bit about being blinded by light is important. Even if light won't kill it, it's something we can use to our advantage."

He was right. She admired how his mind worked, almost as much as she admired the way he looked. He was intelligent, sure, but what she liked best was that he was willing to learn. "What else is on the list?"

After setting aside the pad of paper, Carter spoke, "Now here's the tricky part. To kill a vampire you have to use a blade of pure silver and stab it in the heart. That means that the killing is up close and personal." He paused and Fiona knew he had more to say. But what? "I've been in a combat zone. I've seen things I'd like to forget. Killing a man by hand is hard. Killing that monster will be impossible." He let out a long exhale. "But first, we have to find a blade of pure silver. I mean, where do we even look for one of those? An on-line auction?"

"Actually." Fiona said, hopeful for the first time since she heard Dominic scream. "I know exactly where to look."

"You do? Where?"

"I have one."

"You have a silver sword?" Carter asked, his tone

incredulous.

"It's not a sword, but smaller. A dagger, I guess you'd call it. I'm not even sure where it came from, I've just always had the knife." Her words weren't exactly true. One day, not long after Carter visited Ancient Oaks, Fiona found it under her pillow. Since that morning, she kept the blade a secret—telling no one, not even Lana or Porter.

It was more than a random dagger showing up in her bedroom, although that was plenty. The knife pulsated with a magic and for years, Fiona feared she was cursed.

Carter stepped forward. "Can I see it?"

Her stomach twisted. Was she really about the share such a powerful tool? Then again, if they wanted to defeat the vampire, did she have any other choice?

"Come with me," she said, leading him to the bookcase at the back wall. Fiona found the latch without looking—second volume from the end, third shelf. She pressed the spine forward and down. There was pressure and then she heard the *click*.

Fiona pushed the door open. The hidden room was black as pitch.

"Wait," said Carter. He stood behind her, so close that his breath washed over her hair.

"What is it?" she asked.

"This room is the perfect place for the vampire to hide."

Damn. He was right.

He asked, "Where's the light switch?"

"There's no overhead light, just a lamp. It's on the desk."

"You stay here," he said. "I'll go."

"No," she said.

Fiona cupped her palms, setting one atop the other. Could she still manage this spell? A current of energy swept by her fingers and collected in her palms. Fiona's head began to ache. Her vision blurred and her eyes watered. The throbbing pain in her head grew until she swore that her skull was being cleaved in two. Yet the magic swirled in her palms, growing until it glowed. She willed it into a ball of blue light. It wasn't much, but it was enough so they could see into the room she used as her office.

Fiona said, "We can go together."

Holding the ball high in the air, they crossed the small room. Carter fumbled with the switch before turning on the lamp. A pool of golden light spilled off the desk and illuminated the room.

"Do you notice anything different?" Carter asked. "Anything misplaced? Or missing?"

The walls were covered in teal paper with a paisley pattern. Tucked into a corner, a set of stairs led to her apartment on the second floor. The rug, a woven oriental carpet, was frayed at the edges and covered the center of the floor. A wooden desk, with ornated clawed feet, stood against one wall. Atop the desk were dozens of black and white pictures in silver and gilt frames. In the corner sat a metal filing cabinet that came from a big box store.

A pile of papers filled the desktop. A message she'd written to herself lay next to the stack. Fiona exhaled. Relief washed over her in a wave and she extinguished her ball of energy. Her head still ached. "Everything's the same."

"Good. Now where's the knife?"

Across from the desk, Fiona found the seam in the

wallpaper where the safe was hidden. She pressed her hand onto the wall and whispered the incantation.

"Be it far or be it near.

Oceans deep and night sky's clear.

The door that's hidden, shall appear."

She waited a moment, expecting the vibration of energy to send her pulse racing. Or the heat of magic to warm her palm. Her hand was cold, her heartbeat was slow, and her soul was silent. Fear tightened its grip on her throat.

Had the unthinkable happened? Was Fiona's magic completely gone? Then again, she was still the Daughter of the Moon. Focusing on the wall, the safe that was hidden, and the silver dagger inside, she inhaled.

"Be it far or be it near.

Oceans deep and night sky's clear.

The door that's hidden, shall appear."

Nothing changed. Sure, to perform any spell, the incantation had to be said three times. But without magic, why bother? Rage, bottled up for years, exploded. In an uncustomary act of violence, she punched the wall. Her knuckles filled with pain. "I've heard the saying about hitting a brick wall before." Stretching out her palm, she forced a laugh. "I never knew it was such a bad idea."

"You okay?" Carter reached for her fingertips. He brushed his thumb over her knuckles.

"I'm fine," said Fiona, knowing it was a lie. What's worse—he knew it was a lie, too.

Still holding her hand, he stepped closer. His touch was strong a reassuring. "What's wrong?"

"Nothing," she said, mumbling into the wall. And then, "Everything." She blew out a breath in a huff. In the quiet office, Fiona knew that there was no use denying the truth. "It's my damn magic. It's, well, it's gone."

"Gone? But you made a ball of fire earlier today."

"Yeah? Well, it's gone now."

"How? What happened?"

What happened? What happened? More like *What a stupid question*—even from a mortal. Had Carter ever lost a skill? Been denied a job? Had his heart ever been broken? Or maybe not. Maybe his entire life had been charmed.

Ugh.

"It's not what happened," she said, her tone sharp. "It's what's not happening."

She turned to face him. Good heavens, he was close. She thought of their earlier kiss and wondered what his mouth would feel like on her lips again, her throat, her chest.

Some of the anger left, not exactly disappearing but rather morphing into liquid gold that settled low in her belly. She shifted to the side, trying to escape from Carter and the feelings he'd awakened.

Placing an arm next to her shoulder, he blocked her getaway. Before she could shift to the other side, he positioned his other hand next to her opposite shoulder. She was trapped. Yet, what surprised her the most was that she didn't mind.

"You have to talk to me," he said, his voice low and eyes downcast. He lifted his gaze and met hers. His eyes were more than brown. They were a deep coffee color at the edge of his iris, lightening by degrees to chocolate and golden near the pupil. "If we're going to work together, we have to trust one another."

Did she trust him? Then again, how could she not? "You're right," she said, dropping her gaze to the floor.

"Then look at me," he said.

She was powerless to do anything other than obey.

"Tell me what's going on," he said.

Fiona ran her bottom lip between her teeth, trying to find the right words. "Magic is a little like water because it flows in a current. It's also a little like air because it's always there, just nobody can see it unless they know what to look for. Witches and warlocks aren't exactly like fairies or werewolves or even vampires, who are created because of magic. We're people, exactly like mortals, but we know how to find magic and more than that, we can harness that power and bend it to our will."

"Let me make sure I understand," he said. "If magic is water, say a stream, witches are the only people who know how to make a dam or create another channel to water the crops or fill a well."

"Exactly," she said. She bit her lip again. Her heartbeat raced, thumping against her chest. It wasn't just that she was sharing all the secrets of her world, either. It was Carter. His very kissable mouth. His strong shoulders and muscled chest. It was that he was a man and having him close made Fiona understand what it was to be a woman. She inhaled. His scent, pine and leather, left her tipsy. Pressing her back into the wall to hold her upright, she said, "You know how sometimes a stream runs dry? Basically, that's what happened with my magic. There's no source for me—not anymore."

Her knee was close to his leg. She shifted, making contact.

His eyes held an inner fire that warmed her core.

He moved his hand, and his fingertips brushed her

arm.

Carter said, "Well, like water, magic has to have stopped for a reason."

He was right. Yet, what was she to say? "If we stick with the analogy, I don't control the weather, so I can't make it rain." Although, it was a fact that magic was plentiful during the days that led up to Halloween. If Fiona couldn't harness any power now, what did that mean for her in the rest of the year?

"You created a ball of fire with your bare hands in the cave. How'd you do that?"

How indeed? "I was terrified of being lost."

"So magic is controlled by strong feelings?"

"Magic's not controlled by anything, but emotions definitely allow you to connect."

"What about just now? You made another ball of light."

Chewing on her lip, Fiona took a moment before speaking. "As a kid, the first thing I could do was make a light. It seems that light and fire are the primary connections of my magic. First skill acquired, last one lost. Even making a simple flame is excruciating." She shook out her arms as if that proved her pain.

"I'm sorry," he said. "That must be hard to know who you are for your whole life and then finding out it was a sham."

She couldn't help but see the similarities between the two of them. "Who are you talking about? Me, or you?"

With a shake of his head, Carter gave a short laugh. "I guess it could be either of us, right?"

"I guess so." She paused again. "Maybe you should work with Lana. She can help you. She's a fairy—born with magic, she'll die with magic. I know she seems delicate, but she's not. There was this one time in Boston. She bought a bottle of tequila…"

"Honestly," he said, interrupting. His voice was deep, rich, and seductive, like the first bite of dark chocolate. "I'd rather work with you."

"I just told you, I'm not magical. I can't help."

"And I just told you." Carter moved closer, erasing the distance between them. "You're the one I want."

Chapter 7

Fiona had come into her office for one important reason. She needed to get the dagger, which she'd kept hidden for decades. It was the only thing that could be used to kill the vampire. Until the vampire in the woods was dead, nobody in Ancient Oaks was safe. She had a town to protect. She couldn't be distracted by a romance.

Yet, she was very distracted by Carter Balan.

Until now, Fiona hadn't let a physical relationship develop beyond the single kiss. Yet, every time Carter was near, she wanted more. For the first time in years, she wanted to be with a man because she knew that in taking him as a lover, she would somehow be complete.

Carter was close. His lips were kissable, and his body looked as if it were created to give a woman pleasure. Fiona's mouth was parched. Her fingertips itched with the need to touch him. The room was silent, save for the whisper of their breathing.

Fiona gave into her desire and pressed her palms onto Carter's chest. His heartbeat, strong and steady, resonated against her hands before echoing throughout her body. Standing on tiptoe, she placed her mouth on his. At first, the kiss was chaste, almost pure. Then the kiss became deeper and was no longer innocent.

All of the worry about her magic, her concern about her place in the community, and consternation for having a life, but not a future—simply melted away. For the first time in a long while, Fiona just let go.

Wrapping his arms around her waist, Carter pulled her into an embrace. His mouth was on hers. She sighed, opening herself to him. Running her hands over his chest, she found his nipples and teased them through the fabric of his shirt. He growled and the sound vibrated through Fiona until she felt it in the soles of her feet.

"Being with you drives me wild," he said, nipping at her earlobe. "Touching you. Kissing you. Tasting you."

An electric charge danced along her skin. She laced her finger through his. "You said that I drive you wild. What else do you want?"

"It's not about me." Carter traced her arm with his fingertips. "What is it that you want?"

Her heartbeat raced. She wanted to take Carter as her lover so badly that she could taste it. Yet, Fiona could still move away from Carter—physically and emotionally. The retreat would keep her safe, like always.

But was that what she wanted? To be safe? Most of the time, safety was exactly what Fiona wanted. What about now?

What did she want? Then again, Fiona knew even without asking.

"You," she said. "I want you."

He pulled her closer and pressed his mouth to hers. Tongues. Teeth. Mouth. Lips.

She was awash in sensations, yet there was more to feel. More to explore. She ran her fingers through the silk of his hair. He moved his mouth to her throat and nipped the soft skin where neck and shoulder met. Pleasure mixed with pain, and she moaned. "Carter. Oh, Carter."

With his mouth still on her neck, he moved his hand to her waist and worked his fingers inside her sweater. He ran his palm across her abdomen, then higher to her ribs. His touch branded her skin. Arching her back, she offered herself to his caresses. Carter slipped his fingers inside her bra and twisted her nipple between finger and thumb. She threw her head back and closed her eyes, giving in fully to the sensations.

He lifted her sweater, exposing her skin to the cool air of the room. Yet, a fire burned inside of Fiona. She wanted to get rid of her clothes—and now. She struggled out of her top and threw it to the floor. Pulling down the cups of her bra, Carter dipped his head to her breasts and traced each areola with his tongue.

An ache gathered in her middle, spreading outward. She was consumed by the keen pain of a desire, that had been too long ignored. She needed to feel his skin next to hers.

"Fair is fair," she said, her tone teasing. "I can't be topless while you're fully dressed." She undid the top button of his shirt, exposing a bit of his firm chest. Fiona licked the salt from his skin.

He sucked in a breath through his teeth. "You really do like driving me mad, don't you?"

"You like this?" asked Fiona. Another button undone. Another quick lick to his chest. "What else drives you mad?"

"You're moving in the right direction," he said. "That's for sure."

"What do you want me to do?" she asked, partly teasing and partly wanting to know what Carter liked best.

He stripped out of his shirt. His pecs were hard, and

the muscles of his abdomen were well-defined. Dark hair covered his chest, before narrowing into a line at his abdomen that dove straight down the waistband of his jeans.

"I want you," he said, his voice deep and smoky. "I want to be inside of you. I've wanted to know how you felt since I walked through the bookshop's door."

"I want you, too." She stroked Carter through his jeans. He was hard and long and thick. She had been right when thinking that Carter had been made for the singular purpose of giving pleasure to a woman.

He kissed her again and slipped his palm inside of hers. Carter pulled away from the embrace before tugging on her hand. He led her to that desk that was at the other side of the room. She knew what was about to happen next and had no more patience for waiting or words. Fiona skin was too tight, and she felt as though she might explode. There was only one way to satisfy her cravings.

Lifting Fiona, Carter placed her on the wooden desktop. She spread her legs and he stood between her thighs. She knew, he'd fit her perfectly.

Carter lifted her thighs, holding them at his hips. "God," he said. "You're beautiful. Like a work of art."

As he watched her, his gaze filled with a smoldering longing. In that moment, Fiona felt beautiful and desirable. He claimed her mouth with his own while tracing her arms with his fingertips. His touch, an exquisite torture, moved from shoulder to elbow to wrist to hand. Carter slipped his palm between her thighs. He traced her pelvis until his fingers found the waistband of her pants. He reached inside her panties. A mew of longing escaped from Fiona's throat.

She was already wet. The top of her sex was swollen. He touched her and Fiona was rocked with pleasure. Yet, confined as she was in the suede pants, his touch could only go but so deep. She wanted more of Carter. Wiggling her foot free, Fiona stripped out of one leg of her pants.

Carter gave a low growl, "That's better." He slid a finger inside of her and Fiona's inner-most muscles clenched.

Her breath hitched as he began to move his hand. He slipped a second finger in with the first and she moaned with pleasure. Her hips rocked up to meet him as a pressure built in Fiona's middle. Carter used his thumb on her sex and the pressure became a force she'd never be able to contain.

"Carter," she breathed into their kiss. "Oh, Carter."

"You like this?" he asked, his words were hot on her skin.

"Yes," she cried. "Oh, yes."

Fiona's universe contracted until she and Carter were the only two people in existence. There was nothing beyond the small office and the sensations that danced along her flesh.

"What about this?" He asked, lowering his mouth to her shoulder, to her breasts, to her belly, to her hip. "Do you like this?" Kneeling between her thighs, he flicked his tongue over her sex and Fiona drew in a shaking breath.

"Yes. Yes. Yes." She clung to his shoulders and her hips rose to meet his mouth.

Carter looked up at Fiona from between her legs. "I want to taste you when you cum," he said.

Had Fiona not been sitting on the edge of the desk,

she might've fallen over from her yearning.

His tongue was inside of her. Pressing into the top of her sex with his thumb, Carter drew a circle. Faster. Harder. Tighter. Electricity danced along every inch of Fiona's skin, and she felt as if it were on fire. Although, she didn't care if she burned. The blaze grew from her middle and she was caught up in an inferno of pleasure. She cried out as the flames consumed and nothing was left but ash. Gasping for air, she held tight to Carter's shoulder. He stood and covered her mouth with his. His kiss tasted of her pleasure.

Carter lifted her thighs, holding them at his hips.

It'd been so long since she'd had a lover that Fiona was out of practice. Even though a pregnancy was unlikely, she knew enough to know that they needed protection. "Do you have a condom?" she asked.

"Actually," he said, removing a small foil packet from his wallet. "I do."

Fiona took the condom from Carter. "May I?"

"I'd love it if you did."

She rolled the translucent prophylactic down Carter's length and watched as he entered her slowly. The eroticism of the moment left her light-headed and breathless.

He drove the last inch in hard and Fiona cried out with the pleasure. Carter shifted his hips back, until only the tip was inside of her. Then another slow stroke, that was hard and deliberate at the end.

Fiona liked the languid love making, yet she wanted something that was primal and raw. Holding the edge of the desk, she urged, "Harder. Oh God, Carter. Harder."

"This?" His whispered word hot on her ear as he drove inside of her faster and deeper. "You like this?"

"Yes," she said. "Yes. Yes. Yes!"

"What about this?" He rubbed his thumb over the top of her sex. She sucked in a breath as a jolt of pleasure rocked her body.

"Yes," she cried.

He captured her mouth with his own. The kiss sent Fiona tumbling into an ocean of bliss, helpless to do anything other than ride the wave that was building inside of her. She was carried higher and faster, fearing she might drown.

Then the wave broke, crashing over Fiona. She threw her head back and cried out as a current of ecstasy pulsated through her body. Carter's strokes were faster now. The desk shook under his force, slamming into the back wall. He growled once and then, came.

Breathing hard, and covered in a sheen of sweat, Fiona clung to his shoulders. She searched for what to say next. What to do. Yet, her eye was drawn to her hands and the flames that danced along her palms.

****

As a doctor, Carter understood that Fiona's magical abilities were also tied to strong emotions—fear in the cave, bliss with sex. He also knew that tapping into her feelings was a way to reconnect with her power.

Then, there was Carter the man. Honestly, he was more than a little proud of himself. Sex with Fiona had been mind-blowing, for sure. Yet in all his years, he'd never given a woman an orgasm which also unleashed magical abilities.

In short, Carter was THE man.

He had a hard time hiding the self-satisfied look from his face. Grabbing a handful of tissues from the desk, he turned his back and took care of the condom. A wastebasket sat in the corner, and he threw away the ball of tissues. By the time he turned around, Fiona was fully dressed again, the flames in her hands were gone.

Buttoning the fly of his jeans, he inclined his head toward Fiona. "Looks like your magic's working again."

"It does. Let's see if I can get the safe open." Fiona placed her hand on the back wall. She inhaled. Exhaled. A golden light traced a rectangle in the wallpaper.

"Be it far or be it near.

Oceans deep and night sky's clear.

The door that's hidden, shall appear."

A gust of wind filled the small office. Was that the current of magic Fiona had mentioned?

She repeated the words of her spell, "Be it far or be it near.

Oceans deep and night sky's clear.

The door that's hidden, shall appear."

A seam in the wallpaper glowed brighter.

Fiona drew in a deep breath.

"Be it far or be it near.

Oceans deep and night sky's clear.

The door that's hidden, shall appear."

The light became a door that slowly swung open.

Carter stepped closer and peered inside. The vault was lined with lead. Scrolls were tucked into a crosshatching of wooden cubbies. A ruby, the size of baby's fist, sat in one of the cubbies. The silver dagger leaned drunkenly in a corner.

"This is what we need," said Fiona, removing the knife and the leather scabbard. She held it out to Carter.

He took the knife and his hands turned cold. "I've seen this dagger before."

"Really? Where?"

Dozens of memories came to Carter at once. He held onto three separate recollections. He was seven years old, and alone in his grandfather's office. Sitting in the old leather and wooden banker's chair, he'd made a game of twirling the seat in a single rotation. At the back of the desk, inside a glass case, sat the knife. He knew it wasn't to be touched, but he reached for it all the same. Carter lifted the glass at the same moment his grandfather came into the office.

"That's not for you, my boy." He put the case back together. "Not yet."

Then, Carter was ten and his grandfather let him hold the knife for the first time.

"As you grow, I can teach you how to use this knife. I'll teach you what it means to be a Balan."

Then he was 13 years old, sitting in the passenger seat as his grandfather drove through a thick forest. The knife lay on Carter's lap as he looked out the window. A sign stood on the side of the road. Ancient Oaks. Three miles.

"One day," said his grandfather, while turning the car onto the narrow lane. "The knife will be yours. You'll keep this safe for me, right?"

"Yessir," Carter had said.

A soft hand on his shoulder drew Carter from the past. Fiona stood next to him. "Carter are you okay?"

"Yeah. I." He wiped a hand down his face. "I'm fine."

"The knife, you said you've seen it before. Where?"

"It's my grandfather's." Carter's eyes burned with an unexpected pang of sadness and regret. "He had this with him when he brought me to Ancient Oaks. Then again, that brings up a very interesting question."

"Which is what?"

"Why is it still here? Why are you the one with his knife."

Fiona scraped her teeth over her bottom lip. It was a gesture he'd seen more than once and what's more, he knew that she was trying to make a decision. Yet, what was she trying to decide? Was there something she wanted to tell him?

Before either one of them could speak. The lamp on the desk flickered once. The lightbulb exploded with a pop. Then, the room was plunged into total darkness.

****

Fiona stood in her small office, unable to see anything. No, that wasn't true. The bookcase door was open, the store beyond was a charcoal gray set against the windowless room of black. Bringing her palms together she focused her mind's eye on flames. She felt nothing, not even a whisper of power.

Without question, having sex with Carter had helped Fiona reconnect with her magic. But was it only enough for one spell?

"Carter?" she called out, her voice a squeak. Clearing her throat, she tried again. "Carter. Are you there?"

"I'm here." The rustling sound of movement preceded his warm hand on her arm. "I think the lightbulb burst."

"It's more than that. The store's dark, too."

"A blown fuse?"

"Maybe," she said, her words swallowed by the darkness. Then again, it was more than a little suspect that the lights would go out on tonight of all nights. "Let's look outside. At least we'll know if more than this

107

building lost electricity."

Carter's hand slipped from her arm to her palm. Intertwining her fingers with his, she pulled him toward the door. The bookstore was just as they left it. Cleared of nearly every edition, the shelves now sat bare. The floor, however, was covered with volumes. The large windows overlooked Main Street and let in the gray haze of night. Yet, the road was dark.

There were no lights across the street at the candy store. There were none down the block at the diner. The non-denominational church and the inn were dark. Even the streetlamps, all on wrought iron posts, were off.

With her vision accustomed to the dark, Fiona stepped through the gauntlet of books. Placing her hands on the window, she exhaled. Her breath collected into a cloud. She wiped the condensation with her sleeve. On the hillside, all the homes were dark. "The power's out in the whole town."

"What're the chances that the power outage is a coincidence and not connected to the vampire?"

"Are you asking for the odds?" She folded her arms over her chest and rubbed her shoulders. "They aren't good."

"How do you get power in Ancient Oaks anyway? Are you all NYSEG customers?"

"New York State Electric and Gas?" She shook her head. "There's next to nothing that connects us to the outside world. Several years ago, Dominic brought in solar panels. They're on a hillside in the woods. That electricity is sent to a transformer, and well, I don't know how it works, but somehow Dom made sure we all have power." She bit her lip, as grief stabbed her in the chest. "Or he used to do that for us all."

"I'll tell you what I'm thinking."

Fiona glanced at Carter. His profile was nothing more than a shadow against the darkness. Even without his features, she could still see his perfection. She wanted to gaze at him all evening but couldn't. She looked away. "Tell me."

"I think that the power's been cut at the source and the vampire is hoping that someone will check."

"I'll call Porter and tell him to stay inside." Fiona picked her way back to the counter and found the phone. She lifted the receiver and listened for a dial tone. There was none. Damn. "The phones are out, too."

Carter remained at the window, staring into the night. "Son of a bitch."

Fear wrapped its icy arms around her chest, making it impossible to breathe. For a single second, she thought of dropping beneath the counter and staying out of sight. It might've been the prudent thing to do, yet she staggered to Carter and looked out to the street.

A lone figure at the end of the block stood next to Carter's car. It kicked the grill.

A tattered cloak. Bald head. Gray skin. And eyes that glowed like hot coals.

She swallowed. "It's him. But what's he doing?"

"I think," Carter whispered. "He's kicking out my headlights."

The vampire turned his head. Despite the fact he was so far away, Fiona would've sworn that he heard them talking.

Then again, that was impossible. Wasn't it?

A black blur streaked down the road. The vampire materialized in front of the window. For Fiona, time stopped, and each second stretched out for an eternity.

She tried to move, to run, to scream, but she was frozen with terror. The vampire pressed his hands against the glass. The fingernails were long spikes. The glow of his eyes reflected on the glass. Opening his mouth, he hissed. She saw the deadly fangs and knew there was no way to defend against such a beast.

Her heartbeat raced and she took a step back. She tumbled over a pile of books and landed hard on her rear.

"Let me in, Balan. Balan. Balan. We have unfinished business, you and I."

Carter, dagger in hand, stepped forward. He pulled the blade free from the scabbard. The knife glowed. The light shone on the vampire's face. With a scream, his red eyes turned purple. Dropping to all fours, he galloped down the street before disappearing into the night.

Fiona didn't think at all—just reacted. Rising to her feet, she grabbed Carter's hand, pulling him through the store and into the backroom. Emerson darted out from beneath a bookshelf and raced after Fiona. She pulled the door closed.

Using feeling more than the silver glow from the knife, she made her way up the back staircase and pushed open the door to her apartment. Slamming the door shut, she engaged each of the three locks. Leaning on the door, sweat streamed down her back. Even up here, Fiona knew one thing for certain, they weren't safe. Until the vampire was dead, everyone in town was in danger.

Chapter 8

Fiona's apartment was directly above the bookstore and from what Carter could tell, the dimensions were the same. Yet, it had been turned into a large loft. A galley kitchen, complete with a gas range and stove, ran along the far wall. What he guessed was a bathroom sat behind a closed door in the back left corner.

A living area was at the front of the room, with large windows that overlooked the street. Toward the back of the room was a dresser, wooden wardrobe, and a bed, covered with a rumpled comforter.

Fiona still stood at the door. Even without any light, he could see that her hands shook.

"Are you okay?" he asked. Of course, she wasn't okay. After slipping the dagger back into the scabbard, he set both on a low glass coffee table with a driftwood base. Reaching for her hand, he said, "It'll be okay."

"No," she said, trying to pull away. He tightened his grip. "It's not okay now and it won't be okay later. You saw that thing. There was nothing between us and that vampire except for a piece of glass. I'm sure it could have shattered the window into a million pieces."

He pulled her to him. This time she didn't resist. He wrapped his arms around her shoulders and held her. She melted into his embrace and her rapid breath slowed. "You know why he didn't break the window?"

"Because you showed him the dagger. The light

111

scared him."

"The vampire didn't come in because it can't. Remember what the book said?"

Sighing, she nodded. "They have to be invited."

"Unless you're planning on inviting the vampire inside, it has to stay out."

"You're right." Fiona stood taller. Carter could have held her forever, yet he knew now was the time to let her go. His hands slipped to his sides. "The vampire didn't come into the store because he can't. But you did scare him away with the dagger."

"I'm not sure if it was the knife itself or the fact that the blade glows." He reached for Fiona's hand and led her to the sofa. "Sit down. I'll make you some tea."

"I should be offering to get you something to drink." Yet she dropped onto the cream-colored sofa. "You are my guest, after all."

"I can handle a cup of tea. Trust me. Besides, tea works miracles. It's the first thing taught in medical school."

"Is that a joke?"

"Apparently, it's not a good one," he said. This time he was rewarded with a small laugh. In the kitchen he found several large candles and a long-necked lighter. He lit all the tapers and set them on the coffee table. "Better?" he asked Fiona.

"Much better." Fiona tucked her feet beneath her, but her hands still trembled.

Using the lighter, Carter lit one of the burners and set a kettle of water over the flame to boil. Within a few minutes he had two steaming mugs of tea. He set one in front of Fiona. "Drink. It really will help."

"Yes, doctor." She took a sip and sighed. "Your

prescription was right. The tea does help."

As a physician, Carter knew that after a patient experienced a trauma it was best to discuss the mundane. It gave them time to process and allowed them the space needed to bring up the incident—if they wanted. Yet, Fiona wasn't his patient. It brought up an interesting question—what was she to him? They'd made love, but were they actually lovers? He liked her company, so did that make them friends?

Was she both? Neither?

Maybe, at this moment, it didn't matter.

"Your apartment is pretty great," he said. Sure, it was a little lame. Yet, he hoped the chit-chat would give Fiona a moment to recover from their second encounter with the undead.

"Thanks. I grew up here. Actually, my family dates to the founding of Ancient Oaks in the mid-eighteenth century."

"Wow. Your families' been in this country since Colonial times?"

"The whole town was founded in the seventeen-hundreds." Fiona sipped her tea. "A lot of people heard the call of tolerance and freedom in the American colonies. As it turns out, it was just freedom for a certain kind of person. But Ancient Oaks is a good place to live."

"It's hard to imagine an entire family in this open space. Not a lot of privacy."

"Oh, the apartment wasn't like this when I was a kid. It was broken into rooms. Pretty cramped and a lot darker. My grandparents lived on the third floor until they passed to the next life. In my twenties and thirties, I lived on the top floor. Then, my folks retired to South Carolina, and I moved back to this space. Since it's just me, I renovated."

"Have you always been alone? No boyfriend? No husband? What about Porter?"

"Like I said, I've lived in Ancient Oaks my entire life. Everyone in town is family. Porter might as well be my brother." She took a drink of tea. "And before you ask, I date. I've had several boyfriends. Some have even been serious. But they've all been mortals and at some point, there are questions that I can't—or won't—answer. That's the time when the relationship ends." She set her tea aside. "But I can't believe we're talking about my apartment and my love life while there's a vampire on the street."

"I wanted you to focus on something else until you felt like you could talk." He paused. "Do you believe me that you're safe, now?"

She nodded. "Thanks."

"Good."

Fiona said, "I just didn't expect the vampire to come into town. That's bold."

It was, yet there was more that bothered Carter than the vampire coming to town. "Let's assume that the vampire destroyed the transformer."

Fiona reached for her cup of tea. "I think that's a pretty safe assumption."

"And today, the vampire came out of the cave to kill Dominic. You said, he's the one person who knew how to get electricity to the town."

She paused, cup half-way to her lips. "Are you saying that Dominic's death wasn't random? Do you think that the vampire murdered Dominic so he couldn't fix the transformer once it was broken?" Fiona took a sip. "How would the vampire know who was in charge of repairs?"

It was a good question—and one Carter couldn't yet answer. "Everyone's assuming that the vampire arrived in Ancient Oaks yesterday, right? That it started killing as soon as it got here."

Setting her empty cup on the table, Fiona leaned her head into a cushion. "That's more or less what I thought."

"But what if we're wrong? What if the vampire has been here for a while? You read the book—they don't eat often. Without a victim, would anyone know if something was lurking in the cave?"

"Are you saying that a vampire's been living in the woods for weeks—or even months—and nobody's ever figured it out?"

He shrugged. "Let's call it a theory."

"I haven't liked the woods since I was a kid. Now, I'm glad I stay inside."

Carter felt that he should ask about why she avoided the forest. Then again, there was a single problem that needed his complete attention—it was the vampire. "If it has been here, what's to say it doesn't sneak into town at night and listen to conversations? Maybe the vampire knows everyone's secrets."

"That's a terrifying thought." She yawned. "Here's what I want to know. If the vampire can't enter a dwelling without being invited, then how'd it get into Tad's house? I can't imagine that Tad would let a vampire into his home."

Carter had to admit, it was another good question. Too bad he didn't have an answer. Then again, "You heard the vampire, same as me. It asked to be invited inside. Maybe it's a bit of a mind trick, where some people are susceptible and others, aren't. I mean, who's going to survive and report what happened?"

She yawned again and her eyes closed slowly. "Maybe," she said, her voice heavy with fatigue.

"You're tired. You should try to get some sleep. Tomorrow's going to be a long day." Carter moved a chair to face the window. "I'll take the first watch."

Fiona draped a blanket over her shoulders. "I'll be fine. I can stay up and keep you company."

"First rule as a soldier—rest when you can. I'll wake you in a few hours."

"You promise that you'll wake me up?" Her voice was already slurred with fatigue.

"I can only wake you up later if you go to sleep now."

She gave a soft laugh. "All right. Good night, then."

Carter sipped his tea and looked out at the empty street. If he had to guess, the vampire wasn't coming back into Ancient Oaks tonight. Fiona let out a long sigh as she slipped into sleep. He settled back in his chair and stared down at the empty street.

He had two theories about Dominic's death—something he knew wasn't a random killing. The first theory he'd already shared with Fiona. The vampire had been conducting reconnaissance for some time. The second theory he'd kept to himself. What if the vampire knew about Ancient Oaks because someone had shared information? What if someone from town was working the vampire? It would explain how a vampire could get into Tad's house if they were the ones to offer a deadly invitation.

But who could it be? And what would they have to gain?

What if his second theory was right? It meant there were two monsters to fight—one who was known, and the other who was not.

A thin line of pink warmed the eastern horizon and finally, Carter let his eyes close.

****

The scent of pine filled the air. Sweat snaked down Carter's back. His shirt was damp and clung to his skin. Fog swirled around his feet as he walked through the woods. Carter trudged to the top of a hill and stopped. Below, was a field, a stream, a waterfall. Hidden beyond the curtain of water was the mouth of a cave.

He walked toward the stream and the fog disappeared. For the first time, he realized that he held a hand in his own. He'd been walking with a redhaired girl. Carter's mouth was sore. He ran his tongue over his teeth, only to find the brackets of his braces.

"So, this is your favorite place, huh?" he asked the girl. Somehow, Carter was speaking the words and at the same time, watching the scene unfold.

She nodded, sending copper-colored locks swinging. "I love coming here."

Carter's pulse pounded in his ears. His palms were slick with sweat. Good God. Was he sweating all over the girl? Did she think he was gross? Was he gross?

The girl moved closer to Carter, and he remembered her name. Fiona. "I think this place is romantic," she added.

Was he really in a romantic place with a pretty girl? What was he supposed to do next? His gaze was locked, laser-focused, on her lips. He wanted to kiss her. To touch her. Did she want that, too? The health teacher in middle school said everyone had to ask for permission first, kiss later. But what was he supposed to say?

Carter tried to find the words, but his heart pounded against his ribs and his stomach dropped, like the first big drop on a roller coaster.

The sun slipped below the horizon, leaving them standing in the shadows.

Fiona pursed her lips and closed her eyes. Carter knew it was all the invitation he needed. Bending to her, he placed his lips on hers. She was soft and smelled of cinnamon and vanilla.

"Carter! No!" His grandfather ran out of the woods and down the hill. He held a silver dagger.

"I'm sorry. I didn't mean to kiss her. It's just that…"

"Carter! Run!"

A scraping noise came from the cave, and Carter looked over his shoulder. The vampire stood in the shadows. He ran straight for Carter and Fiona. She screamed. Holding her hand tight, Carter pulled Fiona toward the woods. Rachel, Tad, Dominic—all younger than now—pulled Carter toward them.

"Run children," Rachel said. "Run and don't look back."

Sprinting up the hill, Carter looked over his shoulder. His grandfather's blade flashed in the waning light. He plunged the knife into the vampire's neck. The undead beast shrieked and fell to the ground.

Blood dripped from his grandfather's hand. His white shirt was ripped, and a red stain bloomed on the fabric.

"Grandfather!" he screamed.

"Take the children, Rachel, and get them out of here. Now." Grandfather Balan dropped to his knees, and then he fell forward.

There was a breathless sprint through the woods before he was ushered into the bookstore.

"Sit here," he was told.

"Drink this," he was handed a glass of lemonade. Carter took a swallow; the drink was sour and bitter.

"What are we going to do, Rachel?" Dominic asked.

"I'm taking care of it now," she snapped. "Call this boy's father. Tell him everything."

Carter's vision grew blurry. He felt as if floated atop a warm pool. Which was odd, because the voices came to him from underwater. "Once he wakes up, the poor lamb won't remember a thing."

"You can't keep the truth from him, Rachel."

"Sometimes ignorance really is bliss. This is one of those times, Dominic. Trust me."

Carter sat up, gasping for air. Fiona stood at his side. Her bottom lip was held between her teeth.

"You cried out in your sleep. Are you okay?"

For the span of a heartbeat, Carter was suspended above the chasm between dreams and waking. Only this time the dreams weren't a product of his subconscious. This time, he knew they were real.

Wiping his hands down his face, he said, "I saw it all. I know what happened to my grandfather."

"You do?" Fiona tucked a lock of hair behind her ear. "I mean, that's great that you figured it out."

"I just have one question, Fiona." Carter was rigid with fury. "When were you going to tell me that we'd met before? When were you going to tell me what really happened?"

****

Fiona knew this moment would come. Eventually, Carter would remember his time in Ancient Oaks. The fact that his memories were fighting to the surface was what brought him to town in the first place. Yet, as he looked at her—his eyes filled with rage—she didn't know exactly what to say.

He began, "I know we met before yesterday. You were with me in the glade and said nothing." His last word had the sharp edge of an accusation.

Fiona swallowed. Sure, she expected him to upset but not this mad. "Your memories were altered or removed."

"You said nothing." He repeated, fury in every syllable. "In all this time."

Standing taller, she rolled back her shoulders. Did he really want this fight? It seemed so. Well, then, Fiona wasn't about to back down. "All this time," she echoed. "It's not like I've known you for very long. It's not like I even knew if I could trust you."

"It was Rachel. What in the hell did she do to me?"

"It's a spell and usually some herbs. It's something that's done—harmless really."

"Harmless?" He snorted. "How is covering up what happened to my grandfather harmless?"

Fiona sucked in a breath. "Covering up? I don't know what you're talking about."

"Oh, it's always secrets with you, isn't it? How'd you get his dagger? And be honest this time."

As if she's been sucked into a raging river, Fiona felt like she was being dragged along with the current. "I knew who you were the minute you said your name. Afterall, you were the first boy I ever kissed."

He rose from the chair and leaned on the window frame. The morning sun shone on him, turning his bronze complexion golden. His hair was mussed, and the beginnings of a beard covered his cheeks and chin. How could she stay mad when he looked so damned appealing?

"What about the dagger?" he asked. This time, his tone wasn't filled with enmity.

"I told you. I don't remember how it came to me." She continued, sharing the part that she hadn't told him last night. "I woke up one morning and it was under my pillow. I could tell that there was something wrong with it, but I was too afraid to throw it away. I've just kept it hidden. I didn't know it belonged to your grandfather— I swear."

"And the fact that a vampire was in the cave thirty years ago? When were you going to tell me about that?" He pinned Fiona with his glare.

She stepped back. "You and I are having different conversations, Carter." Her hands began to shake, and she thought she understood why. Tucking her palms into her armpits, she drew in a breath. "I'll admit to knowing who you are. I'll also admit that I can see." She glanced at him from her side eye. The fog of confusion was gone. She tried again, "I'll admit that I *could* see the spell blocking your memories. But other than you and I spending a day together while we were kids, there's nothing else I'm hiding."

"What do you remember about the glade."

Fiona had slept for several hours, yet now she was exhausted. She dropped into the chair Carter had just vacated. "I remember the sunset. You were holding my hand. I wanted you to kiss me." She gave a short laugh. "I didn't think you would, so I closed my eyes and puckered up. You took the hint." She shrugged. But there was more. Like a penny on the floor, some of her own memories were just beyond reach. She heard rushing water and a scream. Her pulse raced. "What did you remember?"

"A lot," said Carter. "I think we both need to talk to Rachel. She's the one who knows what's going on."

****

Carter stood by the window and looked down on the street. The sun shone over the mountaintops, bathing the town in hazing morning light. Ancient Oaks was a charming place, the kind of town where he'd always wanted to live. Instead, he'd gotten military bases—efficient and industrial.

Yet as he looked on the picturesque view, he could feel Fiona's eyes on him. Blood crept up his face, turning his cheeks hot. He needed to say something. Hell, he needed to apologize. "Listen," he began without turning to look at her. "I over reacted. I'd like to blame nerves. The fact that I haven't slept. And well, the fact that everything I knew to be true about the world is a rather convenient lie. I have to own what I said. How I said it." He exhaled and looked at Fiona. "I'm sorry."

She gave a quick nod. "Thank you for that."

Still, what he'd said didn't seem like enough. "Do you think?" he began. No, he couldn't ask, even if he knew his suspicions were likely true. "Never mind. It doesn't matter."

"Do I think that my memories were removed as well? Is that what you were going to ask?"

He lifted one shoulder and let it drop. "Basically."

"I was wondering the same thing." Shaking her head, she cursed. "I can't believe that Rachel would do that and not tell me."

"Doesn't seem so commonplace or harmless when

it's your own memories that have been stripped away, now does it?" He'd meant to be funny but understood how his words might sound too harsh. Lifting his hands in surrender, he said. "Joking."

"You're right." She stood. "So, tell me. What do you remember that I've forgotten?"

"Like I said, there was a vampire in the cave that day we kissed in the glade. It attacked us as the sun set, but my grandfather was there. They fought." He paused. The newfound memory was painful to recall. "We were rushed away and taken back to the bookstore by Rachel and Dominic."

"I'll be damned. It explains a lot—like why I hate the woods. And maybe even how I came to have your grandfather's dagger. What I want to know is why hasn't Rachel said something to me before now?"

"There's a long list of questions I want to ask. That's just one of them." He walked to the door. "You ready to go?"

"First." She pointed to a clock that hung on the wall. Both hands were pointing down. It's only half-past six o'clock. Rachel won't be awake for another hour."

"So? This is important. She can get up now."

"Trust me. You do not want to wake Rachel. There was this time Dominic stopped by too early. She turned him into a toad."

"A toad?" Carter couldn't help but laugh. "You're kidding, right?"

Fiona shook her head. "Not at all. My mom changed him back right away. But years later, he admitted to craving flies for several months." She shook her head. "Poor, Dom. I miss the grouchy old guy."

"Note to self," said Carter. "Don't wake a sleeping

witch."

"Besides, I need coffee. A shower. I want to change my clothes and maybe even eat breakfast. I'd also like some time to think before waylaying Rachel." Carter's heart beat with the need to get started. Opening his mouth, he was ready to argue. Yet, she stopped him with a raised hand. "You're a doctor. You know I'm right. We have to eat while we can. The coffee and shower, well, those are just bonuses. Because there's something else you know, too."

Coffee. A shower. True, he didn't have a change of clothes. Then again, if he were clean and properly caffeinated, a second day in the same jeans wouldn't really matter. "What else do I know?"

"You and I were supposed to come up with a plan to deal with a vampire. Despite everything we learned last night, we've got nothing."

Chapter 9

Holding her breath, Fiona watched Carter. Her chest was tight with hope and anxiety. Did he have a plan? When he shook his head, she looked away and exhaled.

"We've got nothing," Carter echoed Fiona's sentiments, before smothering a curse behind his hand. The whole night was supposed to be about finding anything that could help them kill the vampire. He continued, "There's Porter's idea of a direct assault. Going into that cave will be a disaster. Do you think we missed something?"

She'd asked herself the same question. Was there a book they discarded too quickly? Had there been a page that they didn't bother to read? "I don't think so. We were pretty thorough last night."

"Damn. Maybe a shower and some coffee will help."

"I'll make the coffee while you shower," said Fiona, pointing to a door at the back of the loft. "The bathroom's there. The towels on the rack are clean. Help yourself to the soap and shampoo."

"Thanks," he said, before disappearing behind the bathroom door.

The sound of running water started a moment later. Fiona stayed by the window and looked onto the street. Her chest swelled with her love for loved Ancient Oaks—the people, the place. What's more, she'd do anything to keep everyone and everything safe. But what could she, a witch without magic, do? She glanced toward the bathroom door and imagined Carter beneath the shower's spray. She could go to him again, make love to him, and perhaps more of her magic would return. Would it be enough? Moreover, was it ethical to take a lover, if he was only to be a means to meet an end?

She didn't even bother searching for an answer to either question. They were both the same—both, *No.*

The town was still without electricity, forcing Fiona to use the French press to make coffee. As the coffee brewed, she wandered to her sleeping area. Set apart with a silk and wood divider, her "bedroom" consisted of a bed, dresser, wardrobe, and vanity. Rummaging through the drawers, she tossed her discarded clothes on the bed. Black shirts. Black pants. Black dresses. Black sweaters and black hose.

Fiona glanced at her unmade bed, now a sea of ebony. "What'd you expect?" she asked out loud. "A rainbow in your closet. After all, you are a witch."

Then again, everything she'd done with her life, until now, seemed ill-fitting—like a sweater that was a size too small. Her vanity was cluttered with wrappers yet to be thrown out. There were also magazines she'd never read. Tucked into the back corner was a makeup caddy, covered in dust.

Scooping up the rubbish, she wondered when had she let her apartment become cluttered? She separated the trash between garbage and recycling—throwing everything into the correct bin. The coffee percolated and she poured herself a steaming mug. After adding a generous dose of sugar and cream, she took a sip. The caffeine buzzed through her veins.

Maybe it wasn't just that her apartment was messy. Maybe Fiona had a different problem. When had she stopped caring about her home? Her appearance? Her work?

Taking the coffee with her, she wandered to the wardrobe and opened the doors. Clothes hung on hangers and true, many were the standard black. But there were other colors. Rust. Salmon. Olive green. She chose a sweater in rust and a pair of form-fitting jeans in deep green. A pair of brown riding boots completed the outfit. She'd set the clothes aside, so she could get dressed after her turn in the shower.

The sound of water running in the bathroom stopped and a moment later, the door opened. A cloud of humid air rolled into the room and disappeared. Carter stood on the threshold. Bare-chested, he held a towel in his hand. His jeans hung low on his hips, giving the perfect view of the V at his pelvis.

Fiona knew she was staring and yet, she couldn't look away.

If Carter noticed, he said nothing. "I know it's an imposition, but I was wondering if you had a spare toothbrush."

Of course, he'd come to Ancient Oaks with plans to stay for the day. He hadn't packed clean clothes or toiletries.

"Sure," said Fiona, dragging her gaze from his abdomen and fixing it on the wall. "I've got an extra toothbrush and a travel toothpaste. You want a deodorant? I have a trial-size of that, too. It's not scented, so you should be okay."

"That'd be great. Thanks for the hospitality."

"It's all under the sink," she said, moving toward the

bathroom. "I'll get it for you."

Carter still stood in the doorway. He shifted to his left to let Fiona pass. She moved to her right to get around him. She stumbled to a stop and pitched back. He reached for her at the same moment she gripped his shoulders.

"You okay?" he asked, his hands on her waist.

God, it felt good to be held. But it was more than simply being touched by a man. She craved Carter.

"I'm good," she said. "Thanks."

She still clung to his shoulders. He still held her tightly around the middle.

"You sure?" he asked.

Certainly, making love to Carter had helped Fiona reconnect with her power last night. But was being in his arms enough to reconnect with her magic? Stretching out her fingers, she searched for the current. There was nothing, not even the whisper of air. She tried to inhale, but her chest was too tight to breathe.

Sure, she'd felt her magic draining for weeks. Months. Years. Now she knew the truth. Whatever power she possessed before was finally gone.

****

Carter sat at the breakfast bar, an empty coffee cup at his elbow. Fiona was in the bathroom and had promised that it'd take her only minutes to get ready. He wasn't sure how many minutes he'd have to wait. Ten? Twenty? Ninety?

Really, if she took all day to get ready would it matter? He was no closer to figuring out how to deal with the vampire. He wasn't his grandfather. He didn't have years of training or generations of knowledge. All Carter had was his grandfather's dagger and a book.

The dagger still sat on the coffee table. The book was downstairs, somewhere in the bookstore. Maybe with a few moments to himself, he should study everything his grandfather had to say.

It took him only moments to find the book and come back to the apartment. After settling in on the sofa, he placed both the dagger and book on the coffee table. For the first time, he noticed that the first few pages were stuck together. Using his fingernail, he pried the pages apart.

It was the dedication page.

It read: *To Carter: May you never need the knowledge that's on these pages. And if you do, may you have the courage and wisdom to use it well.*

Carter couldn't help it. The words came to his mind in his grandfather's voice. It was almost as if Grandfather Balan was speaking to him from beyond the grave. Hell, there was no, *almost,* about it. These were directions from his grandfather to him.

Yet, what was Carter supposed to do with a silver dagger? Then again…

He found the chapter on vampires and vampire hunting.

"A vampire is the ultimate predator. Efficient at killing, it's only aim is attack and destruction. Therefore, a vampire hunter's only hope of offense is defense. Like the principles of Aikido, the force of the opponent's attack must be used against them."

The text was accompanied by a sketch, done in Grandfather Balan's signature drawing style in pen and ink. In the picture, a vampire reached for a man—who in turn, stepped to the side. Even in the sketch, Carter could see the glint of a knife the man held.

"Bringing the vampire closer, allows for a counterattack—one for which the vampire has no notable defenses. It is imperative to strike fast and hard—for if a vampire gets you in its grasp, there's very little hope of escape or survival."

Picking up the dagger, he stood. Glancing at the page, he wrapped his hand around the grip, copying the hold in the drawing. The balance was off. His wrist rolled inward. He switched hands and stretched his palm. He tried again. And again. On the fourth time, he tucked his thumb beneath his fingers and the grip finally felt right.

There was another set of drawings. In them, the man brought the knife up from the inside, striking the vampire in the ribcage from below. As a young military officer, he'd been trained for combat. It didn't matter that he was already on track to be a physician. Everyone in the Army was taught to fight and fire a gun. Yet, this picture of combat was more aggressive than anything Carter had ever learned. Sure, maybe special forces got this kind of preparation, but never someone like him.

He studied each picture. Moving through the action frame by frame, he copied the movements. Bend the front knee. Bring the dagger in from below. Follow the blow with power from the shoulder. Each change of stance was awkward, and his stomach clenched. If this was how he was supposed to kill a vampire, the thing would never die.

Carter knew two things to be certain. First, he was in Ancient Oaks for a reason—and it was to kill the vampire. Second, he was woefully unprepared to make that happen.

"Hey." Fiona stood next to the breakfast bar. "What're you doing?"

She wore a sweater, jeans, and boots. The sweater hugged the swell of her breasts. The jeans accentuated her hips and rear. Her wavy hair cascaded over her shoulders. Her lips were coral and her eyes a bright blue. True, he wasn't a fashion guy, but he did know when someone looked good and in his humble opinion—Fiona looked great.

"You look nice."

She smiled—and somehow, she looked better. "Thanks. But you never answered my question. What are you doing?"

Carter used the dagger to point at the book. "There's sketches of how to deal with a vampire in here. I was trying to figure it out."

"What does it say?" She bent to look at the book.

A lock of her hair fell forward, and she tucked it behind her ear. He recalled her hot breath washing over his chest as she mewed with pleasure. His dick twitched. *At ease, soldier.*

Carter refocused on the book and the instructions. "To kill a vampire, you have to get close." He continued with what he'd learned by studying the pictures. "It looks like the knife should come up from below. Punch a hole under the ribcage, I guess, but I can't figure out how there'd be enough force." He ran through the motions. Bend the front knee. Bring the dagger in from below. Follow the blow with power from the shoulder. For him, each movement was a single action. Yet, he knew they needed to flow like a dance.

"Try with me. I'll be the vampire."

"For safety's sake, I should use something other than the dagger." He looked around the apartment for a substitute. There was nothing.

"I know you're worried about cutting me, but practice with what you'll use. As long as you keep the blade in the scabbard, it'll be fine." She lunged toward him. He wasn't expecting her advance but reacted by bringing the knife up from the bottom.

"Good reflexes," she commented. "How'd that feel?"

"It's fine, but there's something about the follow through that's not right." He repeated the words. "Bend the front knee. Bring the knife up from the bottom. Follow with power from the shoulder."

Fiona looked at the book again, tracking the drawings as he spoke. "I think I know what's wrong. The stab needs to start at your hips and roll through your body until it comes out from your shoulder."

"My hips." He tried again, turning his pelvis into the strike. "I think you're right."

"Try again." This time, he could see a haze shift around Fiona an instant before she moved. As she came forward, he pulled her in closer, driving the sheathed dagger up and under her ribs. Carter's heartbeat thundered.

Fiona was in his arms, and he held her close. Her pulse fluttered at the base of her throat. For the first time, he realized that he could hear her heartbeat, too. His vision seemed clearer. Now, he could see everything—from the fine hairs on Fiona's cheek, to the house numbers that were painted on a mailbox, more than a quarter of a mile away.

Still, the knife was pressed to her abdomen. He let her go. The dagger slipped from his hand and hit the ground with a *thud.*

"Are you okay?" she asked.

Carter's mouth was dry. His tongue was thick. "I'm fine." He lied. "The last time felt better. You were right about engaging my hips."

But had she been right about something else as well, something Carter really hadn't thought about since it was mentioned, almost in passing.

Yesterday, after finding Dominic's body, Fiona started telling Carter about the Balan family. *"The Balan Clan has been vampire hunters for centuries. Sure, there's training involved, but a lot of the abilities are innate. Biological, almost."*

"Biological," he echoed.

"Well." Fiona paused. *"It's believed that the Balan family originated when a vampire mated with a mortal. This mixing of bloodlines has bestowed certain powers on the Balan's..."*

"Whoa, whoa, whoa." Carter held up his hands. Even now, a hard knot of anger and disbelief filled his gut. *"You're saying that I'm part vampire?"*

"It was generations back, but it's common lore."

"It's bullshit."

Until this very moment, he hadn't thought about his undead lineage. Yet, as he drew in a deep breath, he knew it was true. With the knife next to Fiona's ribs, he understood how easy it would be to take a life. For the first time, he saw the duality of his nature. Like opposite sides of a coin, he understood that he had both the ability to heal and kill. As he had the dagger pressed into Fiona's chest, he'd seen into a dark corner of his mind. What's more, he'd glimpsed the monster who lived in the shadows of his soul.

****

A clock hung on the kitchen wall. Fiona checked the

time. 7:27 a.m. By now, Rachel would be awake. Fiona and Carter used a set of stairs that led directly from the apartment to the street. Standing on the sidewalk, she didn't need magic to see the change in Carter. Before, he'd been an open window. Now, he was a closed door.

Something had obviously happened. But what?

The sound of a revving engine caught her attention, and Fiona looked up as Porter's SUV rounded a corner. He pulled to a stop at the curb. He was already in uniform. She noted that both headlights on the SUV were broken. "Glad to see you're both doing well."

"We're on our way to see Rachel," said Fiona. "Why are you out so early?"

"I got up with the sunrise and checked on everyone in town. I know there was an order for everyone to stay home. Still, I was afraid someone would go outside after the power quit."

Fiona had been afraid of the same thing.

"And?" Carter asked.

"So far, everyone's okay. I'm thinking the vampire had something to do with the power outage last night."

Fiona said, "We thought the same thing."

Porter continued, "I guess we're all just lucky that the vampire stayed away from town."

"We weren't lucky." Fiona pointed to the store's front window. There were ten jagged scratches in the glass. A million possibilities for *what might have been* flooded her mind. None of them were good and she quelled a shudder. "The vampire was right here last night."

Porter's eyes turned a jaundiced shade of yellow. He slipped on a pair of sunglasses. "You're kidding, right?"

"It's worse than the vampire just being in town. I

think it's trying to destroy every source of light." Carter pointed to his car, the only one parked on the street. "It took out my headlights. Looks like it got yours, too."

Porter let out a low growl. "Why didn't you tell me any of this before?"

"We're telling you now, Porter." Fiona knew that everyone was stressed. Stress led to tension's being high and fuses being short. What she wanted to avoid was an argument among allies. "What do you want? There are a lot of moving parts to this problem. What's more, we all have to work together if we're going to get rid of the vampire."

"I was on my way to check on the electrical grid." Porter put his SUV into park and the locks automatically opened. "Hop in. You can fill me in on the vampire and whatever ancient wisdom you discovered last night."

"Really, we have to talk to Rachel," said Carter. "It's important."

"I'm sure it is, but you don't want to stop by right now." Porter lifted his hair. A red welt ran across the top of his ear. "See that? It's from a spark of lightning. I stopped by to check on her first and this is the thanks I got."

Carter and Fiona exchanged a look. She shrugged. It made little difference if they spoke to Rachel now or later. "Sure," she said, pulling open the door. "Let's go."

****

Carter sat in the passenger seat of the big SUV. Fiona rode in the backseat and Porter drove to a clearing in the middle of a dense forest. Several dozen solar panels winked in the morning light. At the edge of the clearing sat a metal box. It was surrounded by what used to be a chain link fence. Now, it was nothing more than a tangled pile of garbage. The green box—the transformer—was also a heap of junk. A side panel had been ripped off and lay several yards away. Wires and cables, like entrails, had been pulled from inside.

Porter put the gearshift into park and let out a low whistle. "Looks like we know what happened to the power."

Opening the door, the cop stepped from the SUV. Carter and Fiona followed. The air in the mountains was colder than in the valley. Rubbing his hands together, he followed the bigger guy. A post had been ripped from the ground and was bent in two. Carter knelt next to the sheet of metal. Jagged lines were cut into the steel. Had the vampire done all this damage? And if so, how could Carter ever hope to fight the beast—never mind defeat the thing.

Porter opened his arms, as if taking in the entire area. "I know that the vampire's just a dumb-bloodsucking menace. But I wonder, why ruin the whole electrical system?"

Carter asked, "What if it's not mindless? What if this destruction has a purpose?"

"Like it was trying to draw someone out of their home last night? Is that what you mean?"

Was now the time for Carter to mention his theory? Had Dominic been targeted by the vampire to literally keep Ancient Oaks in the dark? "Looks like a lot of damage. How's that going to get fixed?"

"If old Dominic were alive, he'd have magicked the thing back together by now." Porter sighed and shook his head. "Poor Dom. Without him, though, I don't know what we'll do."

Then again, maybe now was the perfect time to

mention what he was thinking. "There's a few things we learned about vampires last night."

"Yeah? Like what?"

"First." Fiona stepped toward Carter. Just having her near left his pulse racing. "Vampire's eyes are really sensitive to light—sunlight especially but even fire and electric light can leave them temporarily blind."

Porter asked, "Are you saying this isn't random damage?"

Fiona shook her head. "I don't think so."

Carter added, "I don't think that Dominic's death was random either."

"Let's say that the vampire knew to kill him. But, why?"

"We've all been kind of assuming that the vampire's an animalistic killer. But it's not. It knew that calling for help would lure Fiona and I into the cave. Last night, it spoke to us. It knows my name. I think there's more than simply a vampire hiding in the woods."

Porter stared at Carter for a moment, before hooking his thumbs through the gun belt that he wore at his waist. "That seems like a pretty complicated problem to me. Why are you just mentioning that you chatted with the vampire now? And if it does want something, what does it want?"

Fiona answered the first question. "There's a lot we need to talk about, but we should *all* talk. The five of us. Lana and Rachel, included."

"Answer my other question, first," said Porter. "What could the vampire want? I mean, other than to kill and drink blood?"

Carter asked, "What if it wants to take over, or destroy, Ancient Oaks?"

"They've done that sort of thing in the past," Fiona added. "Vampire hordes have attacked regions in the mortal world. All of those attacks have been organized. Besides, they have to start somewhere."

Carter continued when Fiona's words ran out. "If the vampire wants to take over the town, the first thing it'd need to do is get rid of all lights. But it also needs to make sure that the electricity isn't coming back on."

"Okay," said Porter. "I'll play along. The vampire isn't a mindless bloodsucker. It killed Dominic to make sure that the town doesn't have power. I admit, that's an effective way to keep us all in the dark. But how would it know to kill Dominic?"

Fiona said, "That's what I asked, too. First, it could've been in the woods for a while. For all we know, the vampire's been walking through streets at night for weeks."

"Months," Carter added.

Rocking his head from side to side, Porter seemed to consider the notion. "I guess it's possible, but I think it's not likely."

"I have another theory," Carter offered.

"Which is?"

Carter drew in a deep breath, knowing full well what he was about to say. "What if the vampire was given information? What if it's been getting help from one of the locals?"

"Are you accusing someone from Ancient Oaks of aiding one of the undead? That they told a vampire to murder Dominic?" Porter growled. Taking a step toward Carter, the cop's brown eyes turned amber. "I know you're new here, but things like that don't happen in my town."

138

Carter should have enough sense to be intimidated by the cop. Afterall, Porter was several inches taller. The guy outweighed him—and a lot of that weight was pure muscle. Beyond that, Porter was a werewolf, and any sensible person should be afraid. Yet, he wasn't. Sure, he respected the powerful man but somehow Carter's eyesight was clear. His hearing was sharp. His grip was strong. In short, he sensed that he had a power of his own.

"You say bad things don't happen in your town? That's what everyone thinks, until something bad happens. You're a police officer. You have to think of all the possibilities, even if you don't really like them."

Porter huffed. "Sounds like you two are experts on vampires. So, what's your plan?"

Carter scanned the field. The bent post. The metal panel, torn and scarred. He pictured the vampire's bright red eyes. Hell, it had come into Ancient Oaks without impunity.

True, the vampire was strong, fast, and lethal. What's more, it understood that nothing could challenge his primacy. The vampire might be undead, but it knew the gods had created its kind.

It was proud.

Could pride could be the vampire's downfall?

Chapter 10

Porter followed the mountain road and once in town, he drove straight to the medical clinic. Rachel's house was located at the back of the property. Rachel opened the door as Porter parked on a gravel drive. She wore a tiger print robe, and her silver hair was wound into a bun at the top of her head. Leaning on the door jamb, she asked, "How's the ear?"

"Hurts like hell," Porter grumbled.

"Good thing I made you cinnamon rolls to apologize."

For the first time, Carter noticed the spicy aroma of baked cinnamon and the sweet scent of melting vanilla icing.

Fiona glanced at Carter. "Rachel makes the best cinnamon rolls on the planet."

If he had to go by smell alone, he'd believe her. Beyond the spicy sweet scent, there was also the dark tang of brewing coffee. Sure, this wasn't the time for relaxation, but the muscles in his shoulders loosened as he crossed the threshold.

The door from the outside led to a small mudroom, complete with a bench, several pairs of discarded shoes, and half of a dozen coats that hung on hooks. The mudroom led directly to a small kitchen. Appliances, cabinets, and counter space ringed the kitchen on three sides. Above the sink, a window looked onto the lawn and the large oak tree that stood in the yard. An oval-shaped wooden table and six chairs filled the middle of the room. A breakfast bar overlooked a small living room with a floral sofa.

Lana already sat at the table, a mug of coffee in her hands. "Morning." She waved. Her fingertips caught the sun and shone with an internal glow.

"Morning." Fiona wrapped her friend in a hug. "It's good to see you."

"Have a seat." Rachel opened the oven door and twitched her fingers. A pan of cinnamon rolls floated out of the oven and set themselves on the table. Carter's mouth hung open. Rachel still had her back to the table. Yet somehow, she'd noticed that he gaped. "I just hate it when I accidently burn myself getting something out of the oven. Don't you, Doctor?"

Plates flew from the cabinet and stacked themselves neatly on the table.

Carter slid into a chair and reached for a plate. "How do you do that?"

Rachel wiped her hands on a tea towel, before pouring a cup of coffee. "It's magic. I'm surprised that Fiona hasn't explained all of this to you."

"She did," said Carter. Rachel set the mug of coffee in front of him. He nodded his thanks and continued. "Magic runs in a current, like water. Then, witches tap into the current."

"That's it basically. But we have bigger problems." She sat next to Carter and grimaced. "Like, why isn't your shirt clean?"

Carter tugged at the collar. "I wasn't planning on staying the night and just have the set of clothes that I wore."

"Fiona," Rachel chastised. "Your mother would want you to be a better hostess."

Carter sat taller, ready to protect Fiona—even from a slight criticism. "The power's out all over town. There's no way to run a washer or a dryer."

"Why would you ever use a washer and dryer? Noisy things that pollute the air and water." Rachel leaned closer to Carter. "Do you mind?"

"Mind?"

She flicked her fingers and Carter's skin began to tingle.

"Cleanliness is next to Godliness.

Cleanliness is next to Godliness.

Cleanliness is next to Godliness."

His clothes started to vibrate as a breeze blew through the small kitchen. The wind tightened into a vortex that swept around Carter. It stopped as soon as it began. Suspended above the table, was a pile of dirt and grime. Rachel snapped her fingers. There was a pop and the grit disappeared.

"There," said Rachel. "Don't you feel better?"

Carter adjusted the sleeves of his shirt. Where they'd been stiff with sweat, they were now soft and clean. True, he'd been more than a little freaked out about magic at first. But he was starting to see that there were many benefits. "I do feel better. Thanks."

"Everyone, help yourself to a cinnamon roll. Porter can go first because I shot a spark at him when he woke me up."

The pan of cinnamon rolls was passed around the table. For a moment, it was silent as everyone savored their first bites.

"Delicious," said Porter, licking icing from the side

of his hand. "I'll take a zap to the ear every morning if you promise to make me a pan of rolls."

"I promise if you wake me up so early again, I'll do more than zap the top of your ear."

Porter gave a nervous chuckle before taking a swig of coffee. "I'll consider myself warned."

"Please do. Now." Rachel clasped her hands together. "Where do we start?"

Porter chewed a bite of his roll and washed it down with a swallow of coffee. "We went into the mountains and checked on the solar panels. The transformer's been ripped apart."

"The vampire?" Lana asked.

Fiona nodded her head. "It's safe to assume so."

"Plus," Porter added. "The vampire came into town last night. Carter and Fiona saw it on Main Street."

"Then maybe we should begin with what happened last night. The more we know about the vampire, the more likely we are to kill it." Rachel reached for the last cinnamon roll in the pan and pulled off an end piece.

Carter pushed his plate back with a finger. In case he didn't know that Rachel was a powerful witch, she'd hoovered his clothes while they were still on his body. What's more, he knew that she wasn't going to like what he was about to say next. Which meant what? That she was going to turn him into a toad? Burn his ear with a spark? Then again, did it matter? Carter needed—hell, everyone needed—the truth. "We need to talk about what happened before last night."

"Like yesterday?" Porter asked.

"Like when I came to Ancient Oaks as a kid," he said. "It was the summer. My grandfather was called to do a job in Ancient Oaks. It had nothing to do with a building that needed repairs, did it?" Carter paused a beat and waited for Rachel to say something—anything. The older witch remained mute. He continued. "The night before we left, grandfather and my father had a discussion. Voices were raised." Carter paused. Until now, he'd forgotten about the fight. Had they been fighting about whether or not Carter should be allowed on the trip?

Rachel folded her hands together and rested them on the table. "I'm not sure what you're talking about."

"Please stop playing games with me. With all of us. What we need now is honesty. I don't care that you wiped away my memories. Well, I do care, but that's not the issue."

"Who said anything about removing memories?" Rachel glared at Fiona.

"I kind of figured it out on my own," Carter answered.

Fiona added, "And don't you go getting mad at me for telling Carter the truth. Especially since you took some of my memories, too."

"Your memories?" Rachel asked, indignant. "How could you ever accuse me of such a thing, Fiona? I'm your mother's best friend. You've always been like a daughter to me."

Fiona reached for the older woman's hand. "Rachel, you are like a mother to me, and trust me, I know how hard it is to admit if something's wrong. But now isn't the time to hide the truth. We need to know what happened thirty years ago, because it's important for today."

Rachel said, "You were both so young and I was just trying to protect you. It was better that you forget than

144

live with the terror of what you witnessed. Don't you see…"

"Actually, I do understand. There are things I'd like to forget if I could. But that's the thing, the memories never really leave. They stay, locked up tight in here." He pointed to his temple. "But sometimes the memories come out when you're sleeping. Or maybe, they make you afraid of something, like going into the woods. But we always have them."

Rachel sighed and held up her hands. "Fine. I'm done hiding from what went on that day. Ask me whatever you want."

Carter was still interested in the fight that happened the night before his trip to Ancient Oaks. "Do you know anything about the argument between my father and grandfather."

Rachel shook her head. "I swear I don't, but I can guess. Your father never did accept his birthright. He always saw vampire hunting as a curse."

"Maybe that's why your grandfather brought you with him," Fiona suggested. "To teach you about your families' heritage."

Rachel turned her gaze to the floor, seeming to see nothing but the past. "It was thirty years ago. Even then, there weren't many vampire hunters left and those that were still around were older, like your grandfather. But we knew we had a problem—that's why we called."

"Had someone been attacked?" Fiona drew her brows together. "Is that why you called Rupert Balan?"

"It wasn't that a person had been killed, not yet. We found several deer with their throats ripped open. Of course, we thought—hoped—it was wolves. Then, we found a pack of wolves, all dead except one. The lone survivor was diseased. It's then that we knew what lurked in the woods. It was only a matter of time before the vampire attacked a person. That's when we called Carter's grandfather. And yes, he brought you with him." Rachel paused, tracing a whorl of wood in the tabletop with a gnarled finger. "There were maps to study and strategy to develop. The town council met in the room at the back of the shop."

Carter felt the memories that sat just below the surface—a splinter beneath the skin. This time, he didn't try to force them out. He let his mind go blank and waited for them to come. He could remember the day. Hot. Sticky. Not a cloud in the sky. He'd stood in the bookstore, his t-shirt clinging to his sweat-dampened back.

Rachel began to speak again. Her voice had a hollow quality as if it came from the bottom of a well. "I'm still not sure why he didn't bring you into the meeting with him. After all, you were a young man—not a child. Then again, maybe that was part of the bargain he made with your father. Fiona's mother asked her to keep you company. The meeting dragged on. Afternoon became evening, and by the time we left the room, the two of you were gone."

"We were in the woods," said Carter. "In the clearing near the waterfall and the cave. At sunset, the vampire came out and attacked."

"We were too late." Slumping in the chair, Rachel said no more.

Carter finished the story. "My grandfather attacked the vampire and saved Fiona and me. But what happened afterward?"

"He'd been bitten, my dear. He didn't have any

choice but to take the ultimate and final step." Rachel cleared her throat but said no more.

It all came back to Carter—the circle was finally complete.

He was in the woods. The air was still heavy with heat and humidity, even though the sun had just set. The vampire lay on the ground. His neck was open from ear to ear and black fluid turned the dirt to muck. Blood soaked through Grandfather Balan's shirt, staining it red. Carter ran, but he glanced over his shoulder one last time. Grandfather Balan drew the blade across his own wrist, the dagger slipped from his grasp. Dropping to his knees, his grandfather fell forward, never to rise again.

Rachel was still speaking, "Afterward, we gave you both a draught, hoping to clear the memories from your mind. Your father came to get you, Carter. Then, you all moved to Southern California—a place, he assumed— that would be inhospitable to vampires."

His grandfather's unthinkable sacrifice sat like a rock in his gut. Then again, it all made sense. That is, except for one unanswered question. "What happened to the vampire?"

"Your grandfather killed him. Sliced his throat with a silver dagger. The beast bled out on the forest floor." said Rachel, giving the final chapter to the story.

Except...

"What'd you do with the body?" Carter asked.

"There was no body," said Rachel. "We came back the next day and it was gone. The only thing left was blackened earth. He'd been burned up by the sunlight, I suppose."

"That can't be," said Fiona. "We've done some research. Light blinds vampires temporarily. Healing could take hours, days, weeks. Eventually, they can see again."

Carter paused for a beat. "What we're trying to say is that thirty years ago, the vampire didn't burn up in the sunlight."

"Surely having it's throat slit killed the creature." Rachel's voice was filled with alarm. "We went back in the morning. If it didn't burn in the sun, where was it?"

"You're saying it might have survived the attack?" Porter asked. "Is that even possible?"

"Maybe the vampire flew away," Lana suggested.

"Vampires can climb and jump. They're nimble." Carter remembered the vampire moving two blocks in the blink of an eye. "They're quick, but they don't have the power of flight."

"They can't fly?" Lana snorted. "No wonder they're dead, except one."

"Lana makes a good point, there's only one vampire left. How were the other's killed?"

"A knife to the chest." Carter paused. "Correction, only a blade of pure silver to the heart, will kill a vampire."

Fiona took a bite of her cinnamon roll. "And we do have a silver dagger, so that box has been checked." She continued, "After that, the vampire's head has to cut off. Then, the whole body has to be burned. The ashes can be mixed with red wine as a cure for vampire venom."

"I'm part wolf and will eat damn near anything," said Porter. "Even that sounds disgusting to me."

Rachel said, "Let's get back to this vampire. What're you two thinking? Is this the same one from years ago? Has it been living in the cave for three decades?"

"It makes sense," Carter began. He then spent a few minutes outlining his theory about Dominic's death being a planned murder, just so Ancient Oaks would be without electricity. If there were no lights in town, the undead could move freely at night. Moreover, it would also explain Tad's kidnapping. Certainly, Porter, Fiona, Lana, and Rachel would go into the cave to save their friend. Without the town leaders, the rest of the inhabitants would be easy pickings.

"You think everything that happened is organized?" Rachel said, to clarify. "And if so, to what ends?"

"I have no idea what the vampire plans to do next, but I do know we can't wait for him to make the next move."

Porter rubbed his hands together. "All right, Doc. It sounds like you have a plan."

Carter hated to it admit it. He didn't know how to kill the vampire and that was his ultimate failure. "Sorry," he said. "But I've got nothing."

****

Fiona's fingertip tingled as adrenaline buzzed through her veins. Carter might not have thought up a plan, but together they'd found all the pieces. And she just completed the puzzle.

She began, "We all agree that we can't fight the vampire in his own lair. But, what if it's on our turf? What if we get the vampire to come into town?"

"Bring him into Ancient Oaks," Lana echoed. "Are you crazy?"

"I agree with Lana," said Rachel. "People would get hurt."

"Hear me out. First, we have to evacuate the town. I dunno, put everyone on a bus and take them to the farm."

The farm, twenty miles from town, was where all of Ancient Oak's food was grown and produced. She continued, confidence in her plan grew with each word spoken. "Porter, if you could get into the cave without worrying about the vampire, could you find Tad?"

"Of course," said the cop. "Just one question," he asked. "How are we going to get the vampire to leave his cave?"

"We wait until dark and then, we need something that would draw him out."

"I can do it." Lana raised her hand. "Like you said, vampires can't fly, so he'll never catch me."

Fiona knew she could count on her friend. "Then, Lana will lead him into town where Carter can fight with him—and kill him."

"I liked your plan until just then," said Carter. "There's no way one man can take on a vampire."

"You may be one man," said Rachel. "But you won't be alone. Fiona has the gift of fire and light. What if she blinded the vampire? Could you kill it then, Carter?"

"If he can't see, I'll have a better chance—that's for sure."

No. That's not what Fiona wanted at all. She had to tell them all now that she lost her magic. "Or Rachel could be the one to create a ball of light."

"It all sounds dangerous—well, it is dangerous—but I think this plan could work," said Carter. "First, Rachel will get everyone out of town."

"Or I can be the one to get everyone out of town," Fiona interrupted.

Lana said, "Honestly, Rachel and Carter are right, Fiona. You should be the one to magic a ball of light."

"It's decided, then," said Porter.

What? Wait! Nothing had been decided—not by a long way. She had to say something. She had to admit, once and for all, that she'd lost all her magical abilities. Her pulse raced and the cinnamon roll roiled in her stomach. Opening her mouth, she was ready to confess.

Before she could speak, Carter said, "If we're going with Fiona's plan, then we need to start now with an evacuation."

"I can take care of that." Rachel popped the last bite of cinnamon roll into her mouth before standing.

Continuing, Carter said, "Porter, you'll take Lana and go to the woods at sundown. The undead won't be able to resist seeing a fairy and he'll attack. When the vampire comes out, Lana, you fly back to town. Porter, you stay in the woods and go into the cave. Find Tad." He continued, "Fiona and I will be waiting with an ambush of our own. She'll create a light. When he's disoriented, I'll move in for the kill."

Porter shook his head. "This plan is crazy. Then again, crazy might be just what we need—assuming everything goes right."

"And if it doesn't?" Fiona asked. She needed to tell everyone the truth about her powers, yet she couldn't find the words.

"We take care of the vampire now," said Carter, "or there will be a modern-day vampire horde. First it will consume Ancient Oaks. Then, the rest of the world. If we don't kill this vampire now, then nobody will ever be safe again."

****

Carter stood in the middle of the town park. It was late afternoon. The sun hung low in the sky, throwing long shadows across the ground. His ribs hurt. His legs were sore and sweat dampened his hair. He'd spent the past several hours sparring with Porter. Each time they fought, Carter's speed, strength and flexibility increased. The movements had become second nature to Carter. *Bend the knee. Bring the blade up from the waist. Lead with the hips. Follow through with the shoulders.* More often than not, the larger man ended up with the dagger's scabbard between his ribs.

"You're getting better." Porter said, wiping sweat from his brow. "But we should take a break. There's a fine line between practicing enough and losing your edge because you've over-exerted."

It was the same advice he'd given exhausted soldiers for years. A pair of water bottles lay on the ground. He picked up both and tossed one to Porter. "How do you feel? You're the one going into the cave."

"Me?" The cop took a drink of water. "I think it'll be a walk in the park compared to what you're going to have to do. You saw that transformer and the fencing. That vampire is strong. I should be asking you instead— are you ready?"

Carter unscrewed the lid and paused. "I don't really have any choice, do I? But yeah, the plan is solid. I'm ready."

"Speaking of the plan." Porter gestured to Main Street.

Half of a block away, two school buses were parked on the side of the road. The doors were open, and a long line of people who didn't own automobiles waited to board. Over the course of the afternoon, Carter had learned that many residents of Ancient Oaks never left the safety of their magically hidden town. Most walked wherever they needed to go, and it meant they never bothered to get a car. Yet, what was true for many wasn't true for everyone. Over fifty cars, filled with people and pets, idled behind the buses. Each and every set of headlights had been broken. Without question, the vampire understood that light was his weakness—and had destroyed everything that could leave him blind. All except for Fiona, that is.

If things went well, everyone could come back by morning. And if things didn't go well? The vampire would've won—and the town would be his domain. For next few days, the residents would hole up on the property of a large farmhouse, owned by Ancient Oaks. After that, well, Carter wouldn't be around to see what came next.

Rachel, standing on the sidewalk, directed the people to buses. "The Thompkins family, you take the second bus. Edgar and Olive, there's room for you on the first bus."

"How long do you think it'll take them to get out of town?"

"I don't know." Carter looked at his watch. 4:45 p.m. "But if they aren't gone soon, then everyone's going to be trapped."

"Maybe we should give Rachel a hand."

"Good idea," he said.

"Hey, Rachel." Porter lifted his chin in greeting as they approached. "What's the hold up?"

"Nothing really. Folks just don't want to leave. This town is more than their home." She sighed. "It's our refuge."

"We'll if they don't hurry up," said Porter, his voice loud and meant to be overheard. "This town is going to be their tomb."

The line compressed as people moved closer, but nobody else boarded the buses.

Porter snarled. "Carter, you go up to the first bus. Tell everyone to find a seat. I'll take the second bus and do the same. We need to get these loaded and on the road."

Carter nodded. "I'm on it."

"If you two are going to take charge of getting everyone on the buses, I'm going to check on Fiona. She'll probably want someone to take Emerson."

Fiona. Carter's pulse raced at the sound of her name. True, he didn't have them mental or emotional bandwidth to think about a relationship right now. Yet, Fiona had definitely been a part of his past. He couldn't help but wonder, was she also part of his future?

****

Fiona stood in the middle of the bookstore and glanced at the wall clock behind the cash register. 4:48 p.m. She pulled her hair free of the elastic and shook out her locks. Running her fingers over her scalp, her eyes burned, but she refused to let a single tear fall. A vampire was loose in the woods. One man was dead and another one was missing. Unless the town was evacuated, the life of every man, woman, and child in Ancient Oaks was at risk.

What's more, as the Daughter of the Moon, they were all counting on her to help save them and the town.

Fiona knew one thing for certain. She wasn't up to the task. Whatever magic she'd had during her life was all but gone.

The shop was as it had been the night before. Every volume that had been taken off the shelf still littered the floor. There were also piles of books that teetered in corners. Other titles covered the tables and the counter. She'd spent the day trying to reconnect with her magic by burning candles. Saying prayers. Using sage. Had any of it worked?

There was only one way to find out.

Closing her eyes, she pictured her store as it should be—neat and orderly. She breathed in, filling her lungs. She held the breath and counted. One. Two. Three. Then, she exhaled completely and paused at the end. One. Two. Three. With her eyes still shut, she allowed her breath to take on a rhythm.

"As above and so below

Rains will come and rivers flow

Sun will shine and winds will blow

Books will rise and know where to go."

Was that a breeze blowing past her fingertips? Had she actually reconnected with her magic? She dared not look and repeated the incantation.

"As above and so below

Rains will come and rivers flow

Sun will shine and winds will blow

Books will rise and know where to go."

Through her third eye, she saw the books, lifted by unseen hands while being moved to their proper place. Fiona's pulse raced. Her heart pounded wildly against her ribs as if it were trying to break free. Her throat burned and her temples throbbed. Magic wasn't supposed to hurt. Then again, if it worked, did she care?

For the final time, she yelled, "As above and so below

Rains will come and rivers flow

Sun will shine and winds will blow

Books will rise and know where to go."

The pain in her head exploded and filled her third eye with a blinding light. Fiona grimaced and looked around the store. The room was just as it had been before. Her stomach roiled and the sour taste of disappointment coated her tongue. Swallowing, she asked herself—what now?

It was her inner critic who answered. *"You have to tell everyone the truth. You're a failure. You're old, weak, and useless."*

It was in Fiona's nature to ignore the harsh remarks. Hadn't she spent the last two days trying to get the voice in her head to shut up? Then again, she knew that every word was true.

It's simply that she didn't know what to do—or say—next.

Kneeling next to a stack of books by the shelves, she picked up the top volume. After reading the title, she found the correct shelf and slid the book onto the bookcase.

The bells jangled as the door opened. Her pulse started to race. Was it him? Had Carter come to see her? Heavens, she couldn't help but smile. Dusting her hands on the seat of her leggings, she turned.

Fiona's expression faltered. "Oh. Rachel. It's you."

"Were you hoping to see a different healer? Maybe someone handsome with dark hair and eyes?"

"You know I'm always glad to see you." Fiona tried to smile, but her face hurt. "Are the buses loaded?"

"Almost."

"Good." Picking up another book, Fiona set it on the counter. "So, you'll be gone soon."

Rachel nodded. "I wanted to offer to take Emerson.

I know he doesn't like me as much as he likes you, but at least he'll be cared for until we can come back."

"Thanks, I was wondering who'd take care of the cat. He's upstairs. I'll get him in a minute." Fiona picked up another book.

"What're you doing?"

"Putting things away," said Fiona, despite the fact that she understood what Rachel really asked—*why aren't you using magic?*

"Why are you bending over and carrying things around like a, a...mortal?"

"I like books," said Fiona, using her well-worn excuse. "The feel. The smell. Besides, this gives me time to think and be calm."

"No offense, but you don't look calm to me."

A tear escaped and snaked down Fiona's cheek. She wiped it away with her shoulder. "There's no denying that tonight will be dangerous. I'd be foolish to not be scared."

"Is that it?"

"Uh-huh." She nodded and grabbed another book from the floor. At this rate, she'd get the store put back together by half-past never.

"Are you sure there's nothing else bothering you?"

Damnit. Fiona should've known that Rachel would read her emotions. The old witch was too gifted to miss something as important as someone losing their power. "I'm fine, really. Why do you ask?"

"It's just well, the memories I removed. I'm worried that you're upset with me."

Fiona laughed. "That? No, I'm fine about that. Well, not fine but I understand that you did what needed to be done." She picked up another book and set it on the shelf.

"Can I ask you a question, though?"

Rachel pointed to a stack of books on a chair. The books levitated and floated to the shelves. She sat. "Please do."

"Why not tell me the truth? What happened with the Balan's was years ago. Certainly, I could've handled knowing about the circumstances before now."

"Honestly, I wanted to tell you. It wasn't hard to figure out why you were afraid of going into the woods, but you were still so young. Then you weren't as young anymore and you seemed happy." Rachel shrugged. "I didn't want to ruin your nice life."

Fiona put away another book. "I suppose that makes sense."

"Can you forgive me?" The other woman's eyes shone with unshed tears.

"Oh, Rachel." Fiona moved to the older witch and wrapped her in a hug. "There's nothing to forgive. Difficult times call for difficult choices. If I were in your place, I'd have done no different."

"You will be in my place one day, you know. Daughter of the Moon. Holder of the town's power. Your time, as the town's leader and wise woman, is coming."

Was it that Rachel had confessed her transgressions, and Fiona felt compelled to do the same? Or was it that Fiona could no longer let other people believe a lie. In the end, it didn't matter. She had to tell the truth. "I'll never be a leader of this town, Rachel. I've lost my powers. I'm picking up the store like a mortal because that's who I am now. I'm not the Daughter of the Moon and if I'm the only one who can hold the town's power, then we're all in big trouble."

Rachel stared for a moment before shaking her head.

"So that's what you've been trying to say all along."

"It's hard to admit failure. Defeat. What's worse, a lot of tonight's success depends on me and my magic. If I can't create a light, then the plan won't work. The vampire will kill us all, Lana, Porter, Carter, me. And that'll just be the beginning."

"You won't stay," said Rachel, rising to her feet. "I will. But you'll say nothing about your powers—not now, at least. All of those people on the buses and in their cars are scared. This town needs a leader, and it has to be you. Now get your cat." Rachel grabbed Fiona by the shoulders and pushed her toward the back of the store, the hidden room, and the interior stairwell. "And go."

Fiona dug her heels into the floorboards. "I'm not leaving you here, Rachel. I'll figure something out."

"See, you're trying to take care of everyone—which is what you'll do by letting me stay. Even if you had your magic, it would still make sense for you to lead everyone from town. You're young and have many more years to live. I'm old, if I die tonight then I've already enjoyed a full life." There was a far-off blaring of a horn. "That's the bus. Get your cat and go."

Chapter 11

Emerson, in a carrier, howled as Fiona carried him down the street. At the bus, she stopped. Carter stood at the end of the block. She couldn't leave without telling him why she was leaving and saying goodbye.

A witch, Olive, sat in the front seat of the bus. Fiona asked, "Can you hold Emerson? I'll be right back."

"Sure." She took the cat. And then, "Hi, kitty. It'll be okay."

Emerson stopped wailing and Fiona turned back to the sidewalk.

Hands shoved into the pockets of his jeans; Carter stood at the curb. "Hey."

He smiled. Fiona couldn't help it—the butterflies in her stomach still went wild. "Hey, yourself."

"Getting Emerson settled?" he asked.

Fiona couldn't lie to him. Grabbing Carter by the sleeve she pulled him away from the buses—and anyone who might overhear what was said. "I'm going. Rachel's staying."

He stared at her for a beat. "Why the switch?"

"Rachel wants me to go because the town needs a leader. If anything happens, she wants me to be with our people."

"Okay."

"But that's not really it," Fiona added, quickly. "I'm not staying because my magic is gone. I can't do anything, Carter. If I stayed here and tried to help, I'd put everyone, most especially you, in danger."

"The other night in the hidden room, after we—you know, had sex. You seemed pretty powerful, then. You opened the safe."

She had connected with her power then, true. "I don't have it now."

"Do you want to try again? I mean, I'd be willing to help you out. Of course, it's all for your benefit so if I look like I'm enjoying myself, don't be concerned," he teased.

She gave a soft laugh. "I wish we lived in a world where we could spend the evening in bed."

"It's not just about the sex. Making love really did help you connect with your magic."

"It might work again. And it might not. Are you really willing to risk your life on a guess?"

Carter dropped his gaze to the sidewalk and said nothing. Then again, his silence was an answer in itself. Glancing over her shoulder, she looked up the street. The buses were fully loaded and ready to go—save for one last passenger. They were all waiting for Fiona.

"I have to go," she said, placing her hand on his wrist. "Good luck. You are prepared. You will be victorious."

"Is that a spell?" he asked.

Fiona shook her head. "Just my fervent wish."

Leaning toward him, she placed her lips on his mouth. The kiss was over as quickly as it began. Without another word, she jogged up the street and boarded the bus.

Fiona stood next to the driver and looked at row upon row of people, their faces held many emotions.

Concern. Fear. Anger. Yet, as they watched her, there was one expression she read time and again. Expectation. They wanted her to do or say something. But what?

"I'm not used to being in a position of authority. To all of you, I might be the Daughter of the Moon, but really—I'm just Fiona. I run the bookstore. I try to be kind and honest." She exhaled. "Well, I'm here with you all now. What's more, I won't let you down." It wasn't exactly a rousing speech, but it suited the moment.

"What happens if they can't kill the vampire?" a witch with white hair asked.

"Is it true that Dominic is now an undead?" Her husband, a warlock with a mustache and goatee, asked the question.

"Dominic is simply dead, and as far as the killing the vampire, we have to hope that Porter, Lana, Rachel, and Carter—Rupert Balan's grandson—are up to the task." Dear heavens, was she really leaving all of her friends to face the vampire without her? The bus rumbled forward. The movement sent Fiona stumbling. She held on to the seatbacks to steady herself.

"And if they aren't?" the witch asked. "What happens then?"

Fiona said, "Then we start over."

"Where?"

"I don't know exactly. But wherever it is we will be together, and we will keep each other safe. You have my word." Her hand began to tingle. She looked down at her palm. For an instant, she saw the slipstream of magic flow over her flesh. She made a fist and the tendrils of magic leaked onto the floor and disappeared. She looked back at those in the seats. "Centuries ago, our forebearers came to Ancient Oaks and vowed to live as they were born—magical and free. Perhaps we've gotten too attached to our oasis in the mortal world. I will tell you this, we are now as we have always been—magical and free. If we need to find a new home, we will. I know you're all frightened—I am, too. But together, we will triumph."

Several people nodded and Fiona dropped into the seat. Olive handed her Emerson's carrier. "That was a good speech," Olive whispered.

"Thanks," Fiona whispered back.

Looking out the window, she watched as the sun slipped behind the western mountain peak. They'd done it. Everyone was safely out of town before sunset. Now, it was up to those who stayed behind to fight the real battle.

Fiona's eyes burned and she bit the inside of her lip to stop the tears before they fell. Then again, what was the point? Sitting silently, she cried. She cried for Dominic, who was dead and Tad, who was missing. She cried for the friends she'd left behind to defend their home. She cried for the magic she no longer wielded. And finally, she cried for Carter. In a little more than a day, she'd come to care for him. But was it love? Would she ever see him again to find out?

"It's the bridge," said Olive. "Once we cross over, who knows if we'll ever be able to come back."

Shoving the carrier into Olive's chest, Fiona said, "Take care of him for me. Will you?"

"Of course, but why?"

Fiona stood. "Stop." The bus lurched to a stop. "Open the door." She rushed down the steps.

Olive followed. "Where are you going?"

"Back to town," said Fiona. "I need to help. I need

to fight."

"What about all of us. I thought you said you'd be our leader."

"You don't need me," said Fiona. She'd never been more certain of anything in her life. "You have each other. But I have to leave now and fight for our home."

****

The sun hung on the western horizon, just a sliver of light in a world of shadows. The buildings that lined Main Street were dark, their window were blank eyes that somehow saw everything. Tendrils of fog floated along the pavement.

Standing inside the door of Rosemary's Bookshop, Carter watched the empty street. His breath collected on the glass, and he wiped it away with his sleeve. The silver dagger, hooked to Carter's belt, glinted in the dying light.

Rachel, across the street and waiting in the candy store, was a shadow against the darkness. Once the vampire came into town, Lana would lead him down Main Street. On the spot between the two stores, he'd be caught in a pincher. Rachel on his left flank, with her light. Carter on the right, with the blade.

At the beginning of the business district, a golden mist hovered above the street. It was moving fast, coming toward the bookshop. As the mist got closer, it took on a form. It was Lana. Her wings flapped so hard that they were nothing more than a blur. She moved by the store and then ascended straight up, past the window. Lana landed on the rooftop with a thump. Carter exhaled. If phase one of the plan had been getting everyone out of town, then luring the vampire into Ancient Oaks was phase two.

It meant they were entering the third, and final, part of the plan—killing a creature who was already dead.

Turning his attention back to the street, Carter knew what he'd see and still, his blood went cold at the sight. A shadow crept along the pavement. Glowing eyes, like red coals, shown through the gloom. Time slowed, each beat of his heart lasting an eternity. He opened the door and moved to the center of the street. The beast's complexion was colorless. He had no hair. No lashes. No brows. Black veins snaked beneath his pale skin.

"You stayed, Balan," the vampire said, his voice a whine. "And now I can have my revenge. Your grandfather almost ended me, but I crawled into the cave and waited decades to heal. Even though your grandfather is gone, I can still end your miserable line."

"I wouldn't count on it," said Carter.

Carter glanced toward the candy shop. Rachel was supposed to be waiting for this moment, but—she was gone.

****

Fiona sprinted down the road. Her chest burned with each breath, and a pain gripped her side. Still, she ran. How had she let fear stop her from joining in the fight? Sure, it usually pays to be prudent. But maybe Fiona had been hiding behind her practical sensibilities.

She didn't quite know what she was going to do. Or how she'd help. Yet, she had to get to Carter and everyone else in Ancient Oaks. Running faster, she wondered—what was happening with them all now?

****

Carter stood in the middle of the street. For the first time, he saw how truly unprepared he really was for the fight. Hell, this vampire had taken down Grandfather

Balan—and that man had been a legend.

What did Carter have? A knife, a book, and an afternoon of practice. Sliding the dagger free of the scabbard he tightened his grip on the handle.

"Oh, you have your grandfather's blade. How many vampires do you think he slayed in his life?" the vampire asked.

"Whatever the number, he needed to finish one more."

The vampire clapped. "Bravo. Those are very tough words, spoken with a bit of courage. I like the act."

"It's not an act," said Carter.

"It is," the vampire whispered. "I can smell your terror."

Mouth open, fangs exposed, the vampire shrieked as it ran. Every cell in Carter's body wanted him to bolt. It wasn't about cowardice, but survival.

Then, he recalled the words, written by his grandfather, years ago. *A vampire is the ultimate predator. Efficient at killing, it's only aim is attack and destruction. Therefore, a vampire hunter's only hope of offense is defense. Like the principles of Aikido, the force of the opponent's attack must be used against them.*

He willed himself to stand his ground as the vampire came closer. Closer. Closer. Closer, still. A foot more.

Carter lifted the dagger and brought it up and around. The blade connected with flesh. The vampire gripped his stomach, howling with pain and rage. He flung back his arm, striking Carter on the side of the head.

The blow knocked Carter off his feet. Landing on the street, pain radiated from his shoulder to his fingertips. His hand was useless, and the dagger skittered across the pavement.

"I thought there'd be more fight in you, Balan," said the vampire. "Then again, I'm not sure why you're fighting me in the first place. This isn't your town. Your world. Your battle."

True, the vampire didn't expect an answer to his question. Yet, Fiona's face came to mind all the same.

The door to the candy shop burst open. Rachel stood on the threshold. Her silver hair blew with a wind that Carter couldn't feel. Electricity danced across her palms. "It might not be his town," said the older witch. "But it is mine. I should've killed you years ago. This time, you're going to die."

She shot a bolt of lightning at the vampire. At the same moment, Carter rolled to the side and reached for the knife. The vampire lifted his cape, shielding his eyes from the blast of light. But it was too late. Carter was already on his feet. He dropped his front knee and brought the blade up from the bottom as the vampire wrapped his powerful hand around Carter's throat.

A golden blur shot down from the sky. Lana slowed long enough to kick the vampire in the back of the head. The beast struck out with its free arm and his long fingernails caught the fairy's wing. The sound of fabric being torn in two filled the night, along with Lana's scream as she tumbled to the ground.

Then, the vampire slowly turned to Carter—and smiled.

****

Sweat dripped from Fiona's brow as she ran the final hundred yards. Panting, she stood at the edge of the business district. Bile rose in the back of her throat. Lana, wing shredded, lay next to the park. Carter, half of block away, was sprawled out on the road. The silver dagger was at his side. The vampire held Rachel by the shoulders. She struggled to lift her hands—to use her magic—but it was no use.

The vampire had clearly won.

Or had he?

Sprinting to the knife, Fiona picked it up as she passed. She saw only one thing—her target, the vampire's back. Bringing up the dagger, Fiona plunged the blade between the creature's shoulders. "Drop her, you bastard."

The knife sunk into flesh. The beast screamed, his arms flailing. Released from the deadly grip, Rachel tumbled to the ground. Fiona pulled the knife free at the same moment, the vampire struck her in the chin. She stumbled backward, landing hard on her back. She tried to suck in a breath, but her lungs no longer worked. Her vision went dark. Her head throbbed and a buzzing filled her ears.

"You failed," the voice inside her head said as she crawled to her hands and knees. *"You're without power. What's worse, you're old and useless."*

And yet, or the first time, she heard another voice. This one had a simple message. *You are the power.*

A current of energy flowed around Fiona and slipped between her fingers. The vampire hissed, showing all its teeth. The stench of decay and rot surrounded him.

The new voice came to Fiona again as she struggled to her feet.

You are goodness and kindness and love.

Her jaw ached. Carter, unmoving, lay on the ground. From where she stood, she couldn't even tell if he drew breath—or not. Her eyes burned, yet she didn't have the luxury of tears. One day soon, she'd grieve everything that had been lost.

You are the light, and the light is in you.

"Too scared to run and hide, little rabbit?" The vampire spoke with a sneer. "That's a pity. I like some fight in my dinner."

Cupping her hands in front of her chest, she repeated the words.

"I am the power.

I am goodness, and kindness, and love.

I am the light, and the light is in me."

A river of magic rushed around Fiona, pushing her forward with the current.

"I am the power.

I am goodness, and kindness, and love.

I am the light, and the light is in me."

Fiona's palms warmed and light danced along her fingertips. Drawing in a breath, she repeated the spell for her third and final time.

"I am the power.

I am goodness, and kindness, and love.

I am the light, and the light is in me."

Closing her eyes, she released her power. Light shone from her hands. Her fingers. Her chest glowed and a halo surrounded her hair.

The vampire shrieked. His red eyes turned black. He lifted a hand, to block the glare. Yet, he'd never be able to hide from Fiona's magic.

Carter rose from the ground. Staggering forward, he picked up the dagger and drove the blade into the vampire's chest. The beast screamed, the sound echoing off the building. Then he was still, and the creature's black eyes turned milky white. Carter pulled the dagger free, and the vampire fell to the ground.

"Carter." Fiona was breathless with joy. The light from her hands dimmed and she threw herself into his arms. "You're alive. Thank the heavens."

He smoothed the hair back from her face. His hands lingered on her cheeks. "You came back."

"In the end, I couldn't leave you."

"We need to talk," he began.

What did he want to say? Was he angry that she'd left? Was he finally ready to forget about Ancient Oaks once and for all? Fiona knew he was right—they did need to talk. But not now, not yet. "Soon," she said. "First we need to check on Lana and Rachel."

As Lana staggered to her feet, Fiona jogged to her friend's side. She slipped her arm under the fairies' shoulder and helped her to walk down the road.

"Fiona?" Lana asked. "Where'd you get all that light?"

"It wasn't just me. It was us."

Carter had helped Rachel to her feet, as well. They stood in front of the bookstore. Rachel reached for Fiona's hand as she approached. "Thank heavens you came back," said the older witch. "Without you, well…"

"I'm sorry I left you all, but I found something important while sitting on the bus," said Fiona.

"Oh?" Rachel lifted her brows. "What's that?"

"That the secret to harnessing my magic is having something to care about."

Before she could say any more, Fiona heard the distant rumbling of an engine. The sound grew louder, and the outline of an automobile was visible against the night. Even without the headlights, Fiona could tell that it was Porter's SUV. He stopped in the middle of the street and jumped to the pavement. "I'll be damned. We did it."

"We did," said Lana. She squeezed Fiona's hand. "All of us, together."

"And what happened with Tad?" Rachel asked.

"He's in the backseat. Looks like he was drugged or something. He's alive but comatose."

"Help me and Lana into the auto. You can take us all to the clinic and then, go to the farm and tell everyone it's safe to return home."

"Is it safe?" Lana asked. "Is the vampire really dead this time?"

Carter nodded. "There's more we have to do. Cut off the vampire's head and burn the body."

"Save the ashes for me," said Rachel. "I want them on hand for Tad, just in case he was bitten."

Fiona hugged Lana once more. The trio piled into Porter's SUV and drove away. She continued to wave until they rounded a corner, and she could see it no more. When she turned back, Carter had draped the vampire's cloak over his body.

"Did you take care of everything?" she asked.

"He's headless now." He wiped the blade clean on the hem of the cloak. "We make a good team." He held out the dagger to Fiona. "Thanks for letting me borrow this."

"You keep the knife," she said. "It belonged to your grandfather and now, it's yours."

Carter slid the scabbard through his belt, so the dagger was held up by the cross guards. He took a step toward her, erasing the distance between them. "So, now that we're alone, I have to ask you—what's next?"

"I suppose we have to burn the vampire's body. Isn't that what all the books said? I can set it on fire now—if you want."

"I meant, what's next with us."

"Us?"

"Fiona, you're actually the woman of my dreams."

"Oh, Carter…" she began.

He pulled her to him and claimed her mouth with a kiss. Pressing his forehead into hers, he continued, "I can't tell the future, but I do know one thing."

"Oh, yeah? What's that?"

"Now that I've found you, I'm not letting you go."

Sure, Fiona could've used her re-found power and looked to see what awaited them both. But where was the fun in that? Especially, since she was sure that this was the beginning of their happily-ever-after. Pulling Carter closer, she placed her lips on his.

"Will I have you?" she asked. "There's nobody else I'd rather be with than you, Carter Balan."

Epilogue
One Week Later
Halloween

Fiona stood in the bookshop and moved several dusting clothes with a cleaning spell. The setting sun cast long shadows across the floor. Carter's retirement from the Army had been expedited and for the first time in 15 years, he was a civilian. With no other duties, he'd set up an office of sorts on the third floor of her building. There, he devoted part of his day studying vampires and vampire slaying. The rest of his time he spent with Rachel at the clinic. It was an odd combination of both western medicine and ancient magic, but somehow—it worked.

While staying in Ancient Oaks, he'd been living with Fiona as well. For the moment, the relocation was temporary.

So far, it had been bliss.

It was the night of All Hallow's Eve and Main Street was decorated for a celebration. True, there was magic all the time in Ancient Oaks. Yet the town always kept the old ways sacred. Moreover, nobody ever missed a chance for a party.

Cornstalks were tied with twine to each lamppost. Booths, their awnings adorned with mums in gold, magenta, and spice lined both sides of the street. Wine, beer, pumpkin pie and caramel apples were all for sale. A group of girls, in costume—a ballerina, an astronaut, and a dragon, ran past the window. They all waved.

Smiling, Fiona waved back.

She was already dressed for the evening's festivities. She wore a body-hugging dress in a shade of green that matched the forest, along with thick gold bracelet and tall boots. For the first time in years, Fiona was happy with the way she looked. True, she liked wearing nice clothes. But her newfound pleasure had to do with the love she felt for Carter.

"You ready to close for the night?" Carter had just come down from the 3rd floor office. Outside, a band began to play. "Sounds like everything's getting started."

"It's still a little early..." Her words were interrupted by a tapping on the glass. Tad, the Mayor, stood on the street.

As everyone had hoped, Tad had recovered from his encounter with the vampire. For several hours after being rescued, the mayor was in a stupor. According to the town gossip, he didn't recall the vampire's attack in his home—or how the vampire had gotten into his house to begin with. For Fiona, it left a big question mark hanging in the air. Had someone broken into Tad's house and let the vampire inside? And if so, who? Or did the vampire possess an unknown skill of mind control?

Other than that, Tad was in perfect health. Although, he'd spent several night Rachel's clinic after being rescued.

The mayor still stood on the sidewalk. On closer inspection, his complexion was sallow. His face was thin, his cheeks were sunken and dark circles ringed his eyes. A pair of dark sunglasses held back his greasy and thinning hair.

"Hi, Tad," said Fiona, opening the door. She stepped back so he could enter.

"I can't stay," he said. "I was on my way home and wanted to thank you personally for everything you did." His eyes watered. He blinked away the tears. "Without you, Rachel, Carter. Porter and Lana." He exhaled.

"Well, I can't even think about what might've happened."

"You don't have to thank us, Tad." Fiona reached for his hand. He gasped and recoiled from her touch. Fiona wasn't offended by his reaction. Tad had lived through some horrific trauma and certainly it would take him time to heal emotionally as well as physically. Folding her hands, she continued, "We're just happy that you're alive and doing well."

"As well as can be expected," he amended with a wry laugh.

"It'll get better, I'm sure," she said.

"That's what Rachel tells me."

"She's a wise woman."

Tad hitched his chin toward the back of the store. "I see that Carter's still here. Is he going to go back and live with the mortals?"

"He's here for now. He wants to learn as much as he can about vampire hunters."

"Why would he care?" Tad asked, his voice a whisper. "Aren't all the vampires gone?"

"It's his heritage," said Fiona. "Besides, we thought that all the vampires were extinct before and were wrong."

"I guess that's true," said Tad with a shrug. "I better go."

Turning, he waved once and walked down the street. His gait was a slow limp.

Carter walked toward Fiona and stood at her side. Wrapping his arms around her middle, he pulled her back into his chest. "What was that all about?" he asked, his words hot on her flesh.

"He just wanted to say thanks for all we did." She

leaned into Carter, liking the way they fit perfectly, as if made for one another.

"And to be nosy about why I'm still in town," Carter added.

Fiona pivoted and placed a kiss on his cheek. "There's probably a little of that, too." She paused. "Although he didn't seem right."

"He's shaken about being kidnapped by a vampire," he said. "That'd effect anyone."

"Maybe." Her stomach churned and Fiona knew there was more. But what?

"C'mon, let's close the shop now," said Carter. "Porter told me that there's a booth serving risotto and I'm starving."

"Sure," said Fiona, half paying attention to Carter; half watching Tad limp down the street. She knew that life with Carter Balan would always bring adventure. Yet, what waited for them next?

****

Tad walked down the sidewalk, silently cursing with every step. Each footfall felt as if a hot spike was being driven into his toe. The glare of the streetlights bore into his skull and made his eyes water. He was tired and, oh so, thirsty.

Yet, none of the food or drink at the brightly colored booths held any appeal.

Lily's Place, one of the restaurants in town, had set up tables in the middle of the street. Yellow and orange plaid cloths covered each table. A line snaked from the front of her booth to the sidewalk. Lily, the proprietress, called out as he drew near. "Mr. Mayor! How are you? Come and have some wine and risotto."

Without a glance, he waved away her invitation.

"Can't tonight. Heading home."

It was the only way though.

A group of girls, all in costumes, giggled while running past Tad. He watched their strong legs, their bright smiles, the fluttering of a pulse at the base of their necks. His mouth started to water and ache. Running his tongue over his teeth, he froze mid-step.

Despite the pain in his foot, he began to jog. He had to get home before getting sick.

He left Main Street and the All Hallow's Eve celebration behind him. Breathing deeply, he slowed his pace. The woods were quiet, cool, and so very dark.

He took another step and sucked in a breath. It felt as if a hot, steel poker was being driven up his leg. Yet, the pain in his foot was a minor inconvenience when compared to the completion of his life's work.

It was decades earlier when he found the last vampire—hidden away in a ruined Irish castle on a tiny island. The being was closer to beast than human, yet Tad had approached and reasoned with what was left of the man.

Come to America, Tad had said. There, we'll infect an entire town of magical folks. Those beings—both undead and having magical abilities—would be able to rid the world of the parasite mortals.

The vampire had readily agreed to the plan. It had gone badly from the beginning. The vampire attacked deer in the woods and made his presence known. Then Rupert Balan had been called. It was only luck that Tad was able to nurse the vampire back to health after the single encounter with the vampire hunter.

Giving a snort of a laugh, he turned off the road and into the woods. If nursing the vampire back to health had been good luck, then he supposed it was bad luck when Rupert Balan's grandson had arrived in Ancient Oaks.

The kidnapping had been a hoax. Tad had gone freely to the vampire's cave and allowed himself to be bitten on sole of his foot. It was the only place that a bitemark might go unnoticed. So far, it had. In fact, it was so well hidden that he'd avoided Rachel forcing him to drink the ashes of his dead compatriot.

Climbing the hill, Tad paused. The moonlit glade, the waterfall, and the mouth of the cave, all spread out before him. He relaxed and ran his tongue over his teeth once more. The usually smooth edges were now sharp and jagged.

The transformation had started, and nothing could stop him now.

Walking down the hill, Tad's chest filled with the pride of satisfaction. He'd been successful in his singular goal: to bring back the age of the vampire.

A word about the author…

Jennifer D. Bokal penned her first book at age eight. An early lover of the written word, she decided to follow her passion and become a full-time writer. From then on, she didn't look back. She earned a master of arts in creative writing from Wilkes University and became a member of the Romance Writers of America and International Thriller Writers. She has authored several short stories, novellas and poems. Winner of the Sexy Scribbler in 2015, Jennifer is the author of the Ancient World Historical series the Champions of Rome and the Harlequin Romantic Suspense series, Rocky Mountain Justice and the connected series, Rocky Mountain Justice: Wyoming Nights, as well as, Colton's Secret History, Book 3 in the Colton's of Kansas series. Happily married to her own Alpha Male for 25 years, she enjoys writing stories that explore the wonders of love. Jen and her manly husband live in upstate New York with their three beautiful daughters, two very spoiled dogs, and a cat who thinks he's a Chihuahua.

http://jenbokal.com